ALCINA
AND OTHER STORIES

GUIDO GOZZANO (1883-1916) was an Italian writer and poet, whose name is often associated with the post-decadent Crepuscolari movement. Though mostly remembered today for his poetry, which includes the volumes *La via del rifugio* (1907) and *I colloqui* (1911), he also wrote numerous short stories and fables, a volume of travel writings, and a script for a film on the life of St. Francis of Assisi.

BRENDAN and ANNA CONNELL have together translated numerous texts from Italian, including works by Luigi Gualdo, Antonio Ghislanzoni, Luigi Ugolini, and the Swiss poet Alberto Nessi, as well as numerous commercial projects, primarily in the fields of transportation and the arts. Their translation of the Ruggero Vasari's Futurist play *Raun* will be published by Snuggly Books in 2019.

Guido Gozzano

ALCINA
AND OTHER STORIES

Translated by

Brendan and Anna Connell

ISBN: 978-1-943813-87-2

Acknowledgements: The translators would like to express their gratitude to Professor Edoardo Fonti for his help in deciphering a few rather difficult textual points, as well as to Daniel Corrick, who edited and published the original volume most of these stories were contained in.

Twelve of the thirteen stories of the current volume, as well as the introduction, were previously published, in somewhat different versions, in *Requiems and Nightmares* (Hieroglyphic Press, 2012), in an edition limited to 250 copies. "After a Tragic Vow" is original to the current volume.

Contents

Introduction

GUIDO GOZZANO was born in 1883, in Turin. His grandfather, Dr. Carlo Gozzano, was a good friend of Massimo d'Azeglio, a well-known politician and novelist. His father, Fausto, was a successful engineer, and his mother, Diodata, was the daughter of Massimo Mautino, a wealthy politician and land owner.

As a young man, he read widely, from Aretino to Saint Claire, from Zola to Saint Catherine of Siena. He learned Saint Francis of Assisi's *Canticle of the Sun* by heart. He read Petrarch, Leopardi, Leonardo da Vinci, Oscar Wilde and Goethe—drew caricatures in the margins of Dante's *Divine Comedy* and read a volume of Ashvaghosha until it was dog-eared. But more than anything he was influenced by the writing of Gabriele D'Annunzio and, when he was studying law at the University of Turin, composed poems in the manner of this latter, which were published in the journal *Il venerdì della Contessa*. But the study of law attracted him much less than the literature courses offered by Arturo Graf—an exponent of rather dark, fantastic themes in literature.

When he first encountered Graf, probably sometime in 1904, the latter was already a man in his 50s, who had published numerous books, of poetry, short stories, and also a history of the devil titled *Il Diavolo* (translated as *The Story of the Devil,* New York, Macmillan Co., 1931.) At the time of their meeting, the professor was also one of the principal contributors to the literary journal *Il Campo.* Among Graf's students, there was Giullio Gianelli and Carlo Vallini, who would both go on to become noted poets, the latter, at points, writing stylistically very close to Gozzano.

Graf's own style of writing was very much the opposite of D'Annunzio. Where D'Annunzio was full of bombast, Graf was simple. Where D'Annunzio was self-important, Graf was ironic and sly. Where the emotions of D'Annunzio often seemed false, Graf's seemed most real—and there is little doubt that this latter was a major influence on Gozzano, and the young man abandoned D'Annunzio, though his work would always be flavoured by him, thus making it a strange blend of the exotic and the every-day, the decadent and the mundane. He was fascinated by D'Annunzio but, at seemingly every opportunity, challenged him.

And so Gozzano gave up the study law for that of literature, associated with numerous writers of his day, was looked on by others as a serious young man who never laughed. He read symbolist poetry in French—Laforgue, Moréas, Rodenbach—and was particularly attracted to the work of Francis Jammes. He studied Schopenhauer and Nietzsche.

At the Cultural Society of Turin, he met the poet and writer Amalia Guglielminetti, also a follower of sorts of Graf, who had just published her second book of poetry

Le vergini folli [Mad Virgins] (1907). Their relationship appears to have been passionate, but platonic. The letters they wrote to each other would later fill a volume (*Lettere d'amore di Guido Gozzano e Amalia Guglielminetti* [S. Asciamprener, ed., 1951])

In 1907, his poetry collection *La via del rifugio* [Road to the Shelter] was published. The first edition sold out in three months and it ran to at least three editions in the first year of publication. But he was in no condition to feel particularly joyful about this as, for a number of years, he had been suffering from tuberculosis, and the condition had worsened to the point where he was forced to travel for his health. He went to the seaside and to the mountains; for months on end wore an inhaler mask, day and night.

He planned to travel to America—dreamed of going to Tierra del Fuego and Japan—but his mother suffered from a stroke and, in order to be near to her, he never departed. He had a passion for natural history, studied butterflies, collected them, and was indeed an accomplished amateur entomologist. He wrote numerous fairy tales which were published in weekly papers for children such as *Corriere dei piccoli* and *Adolescenza*.

His second volume of poetry, *I colloqui* [The Colloquies], was published in 1911. Two thousand copies of the book sold in the first year. Requests from newspapers for short stories and poems began to pour in. For the Turin Exposition of 1911, Ambrosio Film, one of the first major film companies in Italy, released a film titled *La vita delle farfalle* [The Life of Butterflies]. It was directed by Roberto Omegna, Gozzano's cousin, and it seems Gozzano collaborated on it in some manner, though he received no credit.

In 1912, together with a friend by the name of Giacomo Garrone, who also suffered from tuberculosis, he travelled to India and Ceylon, with hopes of better health, and wrote articles which were later published in the newspapers *La Stampa* and *La Donna* about various places, some of which he likely visited, some of which he likely did not, as a number of the descriptions bore a marked resemblance to those found in books by Pier Loti and Paolo Montegazza.

But, truth be told, the line between Gozzano's fiction and non-fiction is obscure to the point of not existing. There is an autobiographical element to many of his tales. Fact and fiction, hallucination and metaphor, are blended together so finely that it is difficult to discern one from the next.

When he returned from India, his health had not improved. He started work on his next volume of poetry, titled *Farfalle* [Butterflies], fragments of which he published in *La Stampa*. The project, however, was never completed. He also began to write more articles and short stories, including "Torino del passato" (translated in the present volume as "La Bela Madamin").

For Ambrosio Film he started working on a script about Saint Francis of Assisi, but never completed the project.

He died in 1916, in Turin. He was thirty-two years old.

✳

The only book of Gozzano's prose published during his lifetime was a volume of children's fables titled *I tre talismani* [The Three Talismans] (1914). His other work remained scattered about until it began to be collected in various volumes that were published posthumously.

Gozzano has mainly been recognised for his poetry and for his posthumously published volume of travel writings, titled *Verso la cuna del mondo* (translated as *Journey Toward the Cradle of Mankind*, The Marlboro Press, 1996). He clearly, however, had a serious talent and love for writing fiction, and his best short stories are amongst the best in the Italian language. In retrospect, it also might be argued that some of these, such as "Alcina" or "A Spiteful Day," are certainly equal to any of his more famous works of poetry or non-fiction.

—Brendan Connell

Note on the Translations

THE translations are based on a number of sources, with most available works being consulted; primarily, however, they are based on those found in *Opere* (Garzanti, 1956).

The stories have been arranged in chronological order, according to when they were first published, generally in newspapers and journals of the day. The original publication dates for the stories is as follows:

The Advantages of Zarathustra: 19 February 1905
A Romantic Story: 15 June 1905
The Altar of the Past: January 1911
A Spiteful Day: 3 February 1911
A Dream: 26 March 1911
The Soul of the Instrument: 20 December 1912
After a Tragic Vow: 30 January 1914
The Real Face: May 1914
Pamela Films: 21 February 1915
The Handsome Hound: 4 March 1915
La Bela Madamin: September 1 1915
Alcina: 26 December 1915

ALCINA
AND OTHER STORIES

The Advantages of Zarathustra

"MY FRIEND," he said to me, "you are neither an aesthete nor aesthetic. No, you are not an aesthete and, although quite intelligent, do not have a superior intellect and cannot see 'beyond good and evil'."

"Fortunately, for my peace of mind."

"No, you are not an aesthetic fellow, one of those young men who are both handsome and elegant and with whom it is a pleasure to show oneself in the crowded thoroughfares—one of those young men who are like the accessories of our clothing and that one collects like beautiful greyhounds . . ."

"?!"

"You are not handsome."

"I know. This has been the universal opinion."

"You are not elegant."

"I know. I have neither the time, the means, nor the passion to be."

"Everything about you—your hairstyle, gestures and expressions, the very way you walk—reveals an absolute neglect for figure and form, without the minimum concern for that pleasure that should be a constant ideal, almost a duty, of youth . . ."

"Very kind of you, my friend. Thanks. And so?"

"And so, despite all this, I prefer you to others, seeing you as a spirit in need of illumination, a mind thirsty for truth and beauty, a virgin soul who awaits the seed . . ."

"Ah! But listen to yourself! Keep your illumination, dew and seeds, but more than anything, do not make advances on the virginity of my ignorance!" I stopped, suddenly, placing my hands in the attitude of the Venus de' Medici, hoping thereby to make him smile, using this joke to stop that reasoning of his, which had already become rather tedious in its calmness. When I saw that he didn't give even the slightest sign of a smile, wearing instead a solemn, grieved and dreamy look on his face—only then did I have the certainty that he had been speaking seriously, had, under the pure sun of that June morning, been getting many frightening absurdities off his chest.

I took careful note of him as he walked at my side, in silence. He really was a very handsome young man, tall and well-built. He had always had that same straight profile, those same beautifully dissonant blue eyes with their jet-black eyebrows, and jet-black hair and moustache. But on his face, he had a new expression now, somewhat sickly and disdainful, of a thinker and *viveur*; and a diffuse pallor which I hadn't seen years before, making it more interesting and his overly-classical features less rigid.

Women must have liked him very much.

And he greeted them, of every sort, at every opportunity: milliners, hetaerae, single women, and married ones too.

Some of them must have succumbed to the charm of his aureole of a superior man, a dilettante of unheard-of sophisms; certainly all of them enjoyed his beauty and elegance. His elegance: a black and white chequered suit with a narrow waist, the sloping irregularity of the shoulders, the collar extending lankly up to the nape of his neck, reminded one of the martyrs of the fashion of 1830. It also had other merits: sleeves *alla castellana*—with lapels and appliqué—horribly open from the elbow to the wrist, trousers of an oriental bagginess, shoes that were indescribably enormous, twisted, snub, and, when he walked, reminiscent of the clumsiness of an elephant's legs.

Yet, despite the Panama which rested on the back of his neck, lifted in the front like the hat of a clown, his hair parted into two sticky bands and the monocle which altered his right eye in an atrocious manner and the handsome arch of his eyebrows, and despite all the ignominies of his hairdresser, shoemaker and tailor, he remained, despite all this, the handsome young man of seven years before, and I paid him a compliment by saying:

"Fiorenzo, it's a rare thing that a man who is intelligent is also handsome, but you are."

"Ah, you think so?"

He brightened up, with a sincere joy which he vainly tried to conceal; and, as his tall, dark figure and my own, pale and blond, appeared mirrored in a shop window, he contemplated himself with a few furtive glances.

"Beauty," he remarked in a tone of voice that made him seem very far away, very foreign, "consoling beauty . . ."

"Are you speaking of art?"

"I am also speaking of the true beauty, the great pleasure, of youth. It's a shame, however, that it suffers from the knowledge that the present is but a fleeting thing. We need therefore to enjoy it to its last drop, the whole of it, like a glass of precious wine. We need to give it precedence, to perfect it—to perfect and refine our senses, those great consolers of the spirit to whose joy alone our existence must be dedicated."

"How?"

"Well—all the most exquisite delights of the spirit are nothing more than advantages for them. Hearing, for example, which gives you the greatest consolation possible—the perception of musical notes or harmonious syllables; your eyes which grow sharper according to lines and colours and the alternating succession of shadow and light . . ."

"My friend, the noon-time bells have just struck . . ."

". . . your hands which can slide over the glossy surface of a beautifully fashioned vase, or plough through a thick head of hair . . ."

"I agree, but we must go our separate ways."

". . . your mouth which can linger . . ."

". . . over a properly cooked steak. Yes, you are right—and I promise you that at this moment I would rather have one than anything else in the world."

I jumped onto a passing tram.

As I was going further away I followed him with my eyes as he receded in the distance.

His hasty walk and the artificial self-confidence with which he bobbed his head from side to side on the pin of his high collar—the way he hooked the silver handle of his cane over his shoulder—all this made me smile with a sense of both pity and antipathy.

✳

And yet, I became his friend, his best friend.

I don't know why.

Certainly not because of the already distant memories of our adolescent friendship: but possibly due to the sympathy that attracts dissimilar personalities, spirits perfectly opposite one another. My cold reasoning, that of a medical student, he pitied, as he did my aesthetic democracy, my collars and provincial neck-ties.

Without agitation, I listened to his *pretty speeches* and unnecessary, melancholy flights. He trusted he could make me into a fervent aesthete. I observed his character with curiosity, satisfying my great passion for collecting, and feeling, overall, that it was my duty to bring the exalted fellow back to reality.

Oh my! Some of his opinions about people, the world, existence! It was as if he were looking at things through a tinted, warped glass, apparently with a kind of unnatural vision.

". . . with unnatural vision. But you are *human, too human!*"

One thing that thwarted my inquiry more than anything else in the labyrinth of his brain, was his constant deceit.

It was not deceit in the common sense—low, of words, but a complete lack of sincerity in the way he expressed himself. For example, he had a manner of talking that was histrionic, a continuous flair that for him was unavoidable.

"Ah! But you can't, you don't want to understand," he would explain to me. "It is necessary for our words, our gestures, everything, to be governed by an aesthetic sensibility, and to this all else must depend. I am speaking. My brain comes up with an idea, the idea travels to my lips, forming words—but before my lips can utter the words, my shrewd hearing has necessarily already foreseen the more or less pleasant effect that they might have on my harmonious ears and accordingly modifies them. And so it is with everything. A superior man must govern himself by means of the continuous clairvoyance of his own person."

"And is it in this manner that you deprive your existence of all sincerity and your youth of all light-heartedness, reducing the world to a stage and yourself to an expert comedian?"

"Possibly. To use Nietzsche's words, the existence of the world, and the existence of our own selves, can only be justified as an aesthetic phenomenon."

"You are surely joking, Fiorenzo. A continuous study in artificiality such as this is, in common language, a *pose*, and is the most disagreeable habit that a young man can have."

"Precisely. This study which ordinary people are only able to do with vulgar affectation and which is called a pose and is disagreeable is, instead, indispensable to a superior man who is able to enjoy it to its fullest."

"But this is not living. Look around you. Look at that woman who is smiling, at that man who is talking, and at that peasant who is singing. Do you think that they govern their smiles, words and singing with the inhuman whims that you speak of?"

"And do you think that I consider them to be my equals, to be of any sort of value to the sentient world? It would be a great deal if, in this crowd of people coming and going, there were four conscious and superior men."

"Fiorenzo, you won't deny that, even if in this crowd there are not many chosen ones, there is certainly much good—virtuous women, men with heart."

"Virtue, heart, goodness. What does all this mean? Womanly virtue? Alas! Where has it been hidden! It is the finest example of the inconsistency of that canon that you call morality. Europeans, for example, despise the so-called *lost* woman, while, in certain oriental cultures, prostitution is a sign of the highest honours. Morality? But from the incestuous Babylonians to the asexual Greeks, and through all people of all times, it has been nothing but a continuous contradiction. How many different types of morality are there? An endless number—therefore none."

"And therefore even goodness is an illusion?"

"No. It exists. It's a special condition of the soul that men have symbolised, I don't know why, in the muscle which is called the heart—a particular state of weak spirits, of mediocre souls."

"Fiorenzo, promise me that you are speaking seriously and that you believe what you are saying."

"I promise."

✴

We became even closer friends. And my curiosity and my suffering grew. It is possible that he loved me for my sense of opposition and, in the shrill noise of our arguments, almost enjoyed the solitude of his perversion.

The arguments were always elevated and intellectual, whether we were walking along the crowded city streets, or speeding about in Fiorenzo's large automobile.

Little by little, he confided in me. He had been left alone, without family. When his mother had died, four years before, he had been left, financially, in a delicate situation, but now everything had apparently been put in good order—at least to judge by the elegant and idle life he led.

"... because I was not made for work. My energy is only just sufficient to withstand the effort of a constant illusion."

At this he smiled—a smile so bitter that it filled me with pain.

We were at his house, on the Via Bogino, a vast seventeenth-century structure which he had rescued from the financial collapse.

I gazed around the large living room, maintained in the fascinating style of other times.

On the walls, which were upholstered with beautiful yellow and turquoise striped Empire silk, hung old paintings, romantic or neoclassical prints, and a great number of miniatures in frames of tortoise and gold.

"Fiorenzo, who is that *incroyable* in a peplos in that painting over there?"

"The painting is by David. The woman is Gaspara di Vareglio, my father's great-grandmother, lady-in-waiting to Amalia Beauharnais."

"The other, to the right, is Empire as well?"

"Also by David. It is the Donna Gaspara's daughter, who was a very spiritual woman. Before settling in Piedmont, she maintained a salon in Paris which was frequented by the intelligentsia and the cream of the nobility. She was a friend of Byron, his lover I believe. I will let you read a copy of a letter that I have—one that she sent to the poet's biographer, a fellow who died a year ago, in Missolungi, and which includes many interesting details and in which she writes '. . . *que rien n'aurait pûr être, en verité, plus amusant et plus délicieux. Dans l'intimité il avait la gaieté d'un enfant auquel on donnerait de vacances . . .*'[1] I believe she knew him . . . quite well. What do you think?"

Fiorenzo spoke standing by an enormous window, high and with double frames, from which the deepening twilight almost did not come through anymore. My friend pressed his forehead against the window pane, as if to cool it—against the very window once touched, in another century, by the rouged cheeks and powdered hair of the ladies and *cicisbei*—the same people who were looking attentively at their descendant from the photographs and paintings.

As evening descended, I was struck by the beauty of that living room, large and dark, where the baroque of

---

1 ". . . that nothing would, in truth, be as purely amusing and delicious. In intimacy he had the gaiety of a child on holiday . . ."

the seventeenth century, the affectations of the eighteenth, the rigidity of the Empire, and the sentimentality of Romanticism, had all left their traces.

"Haven't I told you that my little volume is dedicated to a lady?"

"This is bad Fiorenzo. A superman like you, dedicating *verses* to a *lady*, like any common, sentimental poet! Did not the Daemon warn you that you were breaking the *rule*? Follow the admonition of the Despot."

"Don't laugh! It concerns one of the *elect*—the only true intellectual I have ever known. In her, her sex, her womanhood, no longer counts."

We heard slowly approaching steps and an old servant with a big lantern came in, re-awakening me to reality and light.

"A letter for you, Marquis!"

"Ah!"

Fiorenzo opened it, looked it over smiling, almost laughing, then tossed the sheet of paper to me:

"Read it. It's from her, the lady to whom my book is dedicated."

The lady was writing to him from a lonely villa, where she looked after her invalid husband. She thought of the young man, imagining his beauty, and called him by the sweetest names: ". . . and I have no remorse—I have no remorse for letting my soul be with you while I hear Giacomo's laboured breathing coming to me from the other room. So great is my need for love, that it keeps my poor life from declining."

"Ah! Finally! Now at least you will be moved. The situation is one that will satisfy your erotic and aesthetic ideals . . ."

"Yes, certainly . . ."

And he laughed and laughed . . .

"This lady is a true intellectual. The letter is magnificent."

"An intellectual, certainly—and also fifty-two years old."

"Eh?"

"Fake teeth."

"!"

"Dyed hair."

"!"

"But understand: she is a millionaire!"

A Romantic Story

"**Y**OU did well to celebrate the marriage in this room. It's more cheerful."

The spacious room was decorated in Corinthian pink marble; the pattern of the wallpaper was green willow wreaths and imperial eagles.

"It is not the largest, Your Majesty, but the other side of the castle, the medieval section, has not yet been restored, and is rather gloomy . . ."

"And there is a legend surrounding it, isn't that so?" Maria Cristina of Savoy asked.

The few guests who had not gone down to the park approached in curiosity.

The Countess told the story, a few gentlemen smiling incredulously.

"Well, I don't really believe it myself. It is certainly a legend. The reality, however, is this: my grandmother's two brothers, Filippo and Alessandro, who were twins, disappeared one day, suddenly, and nothing was ever heard of them again. I was a child, and can only just remember. The last time they were seen was near the Torri delle Cornacchie,[1] on the south side. . . . The event

---

1 Towers of the Crows.

caused a huge stir and rumour has it that, even before this, others had disappeared in the same manner.

"People claim that a horrible and mysterious monster lives in the foundation and comes out to dine on human flesh once every hundred years."

The Queen and the Countess of Felligno walked to a large open window and looked out at the park.

Most of the young people were already there.

The Countess immediately made out the large, bright-white crinoline of her daughter Sofia on some distant steps. She saw the beautiful blonde hair, parted in the middle and brushed over the girl's cheeks in two wavy locks. The bridegroom stood next to her, his brown head of hair inclined near hers. It appeared as if they were reading. When, after a brief period, they moved away from each other, the Countess saw that her daughter did in fact hold a book in her hands. A great tenderness filled the mother's heart. Later that day, Sofia was to be taken by her love far away.

But what was Sofia doing now? She was walking down a path, reading. The groom stayed behind, leaning against the balustrade, following his beloved with tender eyes. She moved further away, disappearing behind a plinth, then reappearing between the pyramid shapes of two boxwoods, then disappearing again in a thicket.

Queen Maria Cristina was taking her leave.

The servants went down to the park to make the announcement and all the scattered guests made their way back in order to pay their respects to the illustrious visitor.

In the entrance-hall of the palace, the Queen received her homage and had her hand kissed.

"And Sofia? I would like to hug the bride!"

"Where is Sofia?" the Countess asked her son-in-law, who was standing nearby.

"Isn't she here? I thought perhaps she had already come. She walked off through the Path of the Statues with a copy of *Parisina*[1] in her hand, begging me not to follow her. She wanted to enjoy a moment of melancholy. But the servants are looking for her, they must have let her know. She will be here in a moment. Would Your Majesty be so kind as to forgive her?" And the young man bent forward to kiss the hand of the Queen.

They waited.

The servants all came back.

Sofia did not return that day, or thereafter.

A year later.

From Sorrento, where his family had sent him for convalescence, fearing for both his reason and life, the groom returned to the Castle of Felligno.

The Countess had died that winter, so he was left alone, in the house and park of his broken love, with only memories. He lived in a sort of poetic exaltation,

____

1 A poem by Byron that achieved great success in Italy in a translated edition.

nourished by constant thoughts of her who was absent, his mood swinging back and forth between depression and hope. Would he see her again? Would she ever return? Where was she? What was she doing? What was she thinking? Was she alive? Suffering? Where, where? For a year no light had been shed on that terrible mystery. Just as had happened to Filippo and Alessandro, his two ancestors, Sofia had disappeared without a trace. She had simply vanished, in her wedding dress, while walking through the park. Was it possible?

The enigma reached the bounds of the improbable; the young man let himself be carried away by torturing fantasies.

Nourished on melancholy and Leopardian pessimism, exalted by Byron's poetry and heroes, he would with cruel suppositions sometimes find solutions to the mystery:

"Sofia surely never loved me. She must have been concealing some infamous affair and run off in the arms of her lover."

Then he would feel remorse, acknowledging the childish perversity of his thoughts, mentally asking his lost bride to forgive him. The search became a kind of mania, a paroxysm. Even when he was most discouraged, his gaze was always alert, investigating the most minute things: the grass, the pebbles on the path, the patches of moss on the benches and statues.

His eyes were quick, bright, extremely mobile, like those of a feverish person. His hearing became so refined that he would jump back at the rustle of a beetle or moth, as if it were a shout.

He had by this time searched the entire castle, the entire park, the countryside and surrounding cottages. One walk, however, he would take every day, with the same hope: the Path of Statues.

The avenue, lined with statues and poplars, stretched for over half a kilometre before disappearing in a stand of firs.

That morning, when the young man reached the firs, he decided to change his route. He took a path through some fields, made his way over a meadow, and presently came to the foot of Felligno Hill. On top of the small hill, white, feudal walls stood in ruins. Further above, the three Torri delle Cornacchie stood out undamaged, blood-red, just as Simone of Felligno had ordered them to be built against the invasion of the Selassi in 1210.

The young man looked at the white walls against the green of the hill, at the flaming towers against the blue of the sky; then began to climb through the grass and ruins—and his heart was oppressed by the contrast between the sweetness of the seventeenth-century imperial residence, which he had just left, and the austerity of the archaic and feudal scenery around him.

He went slowly, and suddenly realised that, for the first time, he had spent a few moments without thinking of her. The scenery had distracted him. Also, the surrounding area and towers had been previously searched by the servants and militia in order to dispel the absurd legend; thus, they did not remind him of his dear and missing bride. A few minutes later, having come to the top of the hill, he entered, out of pure curiosity, the first tower. The room had high arches and was humid and dark, but from one end a beam of light entered through a small door. He made his way forward and saw that there was a very steep stairway which went down to an inner courtyard. The courtyard was spacious, with an aspect at once cloistral and feudal, surrounded by low, gloomy arcades, and in the middle was a polygon-shaped well of white stone, with a chain pulley made of wrought iron and shaped like a small tree with branches. As the place was cool and protected, the ground was completely covered with enormous clovers and the arcades with thick ivy.

The young man lay down on the clover, which was as inviting as a cushion, and gazed around, absently, in the great silence.

At the bottom of the courtyard, in a thin strip of slanting sun, a large white Pieridae fluttered above the yellow flowers of a rapeseed plant; then the butterfly, growing weary of this, directed its flight toward the arcades, rising, rising until it reached the top of the walls, and disappeared.

The young man, still lying on the grass, followed it absently with his eyes. He then turned around and looked at the wall behind him. A large white patch attracted his attention. It was the area untouched by the mantle of ivy. He was but a short distance away and thought he detected a red mark. He rose to his feet and read on the wall a word: ". . . *of* . . .". The rest had been erased by rain. He looked about and saw stones and bricks on the ground. The word must have been written with the chip of a brick.

Suddenly inspired, he gathered a mass of the climbing plant in his hands and lifted it up as if it were a head of hair.

And the hair he had to hang on to in order not to fall to the ground when he saw the red letters that the ivy had protected:

. . . Yet thus must Hugo meet his sire,
And hear the sentence of his ire . . .

The handwriting was Sofia's, the words from *Parisina*.

Still holding onto the strong ivy, his knees bent like two reeds, the groom was annihilated, hearing the blood rumbling in his veins and beating in his head with the violence of a hammer.

✳

The place seemed to have been transformed: everything spoke of her.

Sunlight now filled a third of the courtyard. The butterfly had returned to the rapeseed with a companion.

He tried to put his thoughts in order.

Sofia! So, Sofia had been in these places which she had probably seen for the first time, attracted by her romantic taste, and had given them her farewell!

He looked further. He went over the entire green wall several times, to find a clue.

He thought he saw a bright spot inside the thick ivy and put his hands within. The thick mass moved away, parting as easily as a curtain, and a large opening appeared in the wall.

On the other side was a small courtyard, enclosed between towering stone walls, at the top of which the sky appeared like a small blue square. The grass came up to his waist. The place seemed as if it had been deserted for a thousand years.

He walked forward, seeing on a white stone in the wall, unprotected by the ivy, that well-known handwriting, faded. He read, without astonishment, since he was beyond astonishment:

> *. . . Parisina leaves her hall,*
> *And it is not to gaze . . .*

"*. . . on the heavenly light*," the young man said unintentionally. His memory, as if awoken by a bell, had completed the line which he had read many times with her.

He had the impression that he was breathing some element which was not air; he heard an indistinct rumbling in his ears, saw everything through a strange veil which made it appear unreal, like a painting. Slowly he made his way forward, through the grass.

The grass was soft.

Was that a cat looking at him from a corner?

Yes, a black cat eating a lizard, tearing off its legs. And what was that? Ah! The tail of the halved lizard struggling like a little snake.

What a dream!

The grass was soft, yielding. But was it the grass that was yielding?

Oh, God, no! It was not the grass.

He had just time enough to take hold of the crevices of the wall, instinctively.

A stone, a huge, round stone, was giving way, moving gently as if on a balance.

Still hanging on, he began to coax it with his foot.

With each tap, the rock moved on its axis: it was enormous, taking up nearly half the small courtyard.

Was he dreaming? Yes, certainly he was dreaming!

But what a dream!

With his foot he added more and more force, and the lid, continuing to oscillate, began to sink ponderously.

What a dream!

But he wanted to look inside, where he had not yet seen.

With every tap, a horrible smell issued from the trapdoor, like the gasps of a man struck by the plague.

Putting forward all his energy, he gave the rock a vigorous push. One side of it rose up, the other sunk down. He took hold of the edge, keeping it in place with one hand while, with the other, he clung to the crevices in the wall, his feet resting at its base. In this way, leaning his entire body forward, he was able to see within.

A square chamber, black and deep with formless whitish things scattered about. In a corner he could make out, apparent due to the circles of crinoline, a white dress, the silk stained here and there; then, in profile, a skull; then a braid, tangled like that of a mummy, and then—oh! but what a nightmare!—a root . . . no! A leg. A foot. . . . Oh!

What a dream! Wake up! Wake up!

He was falling, falling, letting himself fall.

What pain!

Pain, pain! Hip, arms, hands!

And the white butterfly? And the strip of sun? And the black cat? And the lizard? And the dancing tail? And that hollow sound?

But where, where?

Then, in the dark, with his hands in the heap of bones and rotting flesh, his human brain understood.

"I am never going to get out of here. Never."

And he went mad.

The Altar of the Past

THE other day, while standing in front of his destroyed home with a dear seventy-five-year-old lady friend of mine, I thought again of Count Fiorenzo X.

And the lady solved a somewhat amusing sentimental mystery for me—one that had been asleep in my memory for almost twenty years.

Eighteen years ago, I regularly frequented the house of Count X. I was then eight years old, the same age as Vittorino, his grandson. We were at third elementary together in the gloomy school of the Barnabiti Fathers in the old section of Turin.

The friendship between us two schoolboys was born out of mutual interest; Vittorino was strong in math, I in composition; one dealt with the writing, the other the arithmetic. And we also exchanged hospitality during the holidays. To get to my friend's house, you had to walk through the old part of town, which today has almost completely disappeared—a labyrinth of dark lanes perfumed with the smell of taverns and tanneries, rotten fruits and marc, the sky appearing like a thin and twisted ribbon above, between the decayed walls of the homes of the nobility.

I can still see my friend's home. A building that was pure seventeenth-century Piedmont, with a series of immense windows; resting atop the two columns of the entrance was a big balcony with a curved balustrade, in the centre of which was the family arms and motto, and many bellflowers and roses, and many carnations which twined and spilled out from amidst the old iron like young hair.

That was where Count Fiorenzo had his study, and those were the flowers he cultivated with his own hands.

The foyer and stairway, vast, dark, cold and dusty, were lined with granite columns. There was no doorman. Poor Mini served as doorman. He was the faithful servant of the count, who had been his companion of youth, travel, adventure—and he was also the cook, butler, groom, and teacher, and made up, together with a maid as decrepit as himself and a young man who worked part-time, the whole of the house's servants.

A sad place, from which you felt a sense of abandonment, decadence, persistent pride and poorly disguised circumstances from the moment you crossed the threshold.

How many Thursdays and Sundays I spent in those dark rooms, amidst worm-eaten, worn-out and faded things!

When the last line of homework had been completed—done first thing in the morning under the guidance of Count Fiorenzo—we would leap out of our seats with a cry of relief, dash through the large dark hallway, making our way hastily to kitchen, to the great distress of poor Mini and Ghita, who were busy preparing breakfast.

And for the rest of the day, we tried to interpret, in reverse, the rhetorical reproaches of *The Book of Good Reading*.

Some of our great delights, at least among those that can be confessed, were to provoke the servants, pluck the chickens in the coop, shoot the ancestors depicted in the old paintings with a Flobert, torment Aunt Ernesta, a mad woman who lived on the third floor, make our way up to the attic, and once there, lean through the small oval windows and drop paper bags full of water, or worse, onto the heads of those walking below.

At exactly midday the lunch bell rang. We stopped whatever we were doing, washed ourselves and, for table, recomposed our faces with sweet hypocrisy.

If I close my eyes I can still see the vast dining room, see the various figures in the Rembrandt-like semi-darkness. The Marquise Amalia, my friend's mother, a widow. Aunt Ernesta, silent and ghost-like. The clumsy Jesuit priest uncle. Another uncle, a captain, clumsy and arrogant.

And amidst these was that wonderful person, *il signor papà*, the only one who was nice, Count Fiorenzo—a handsome man who was still agile and vibrant, with thick silver hair, and the perfect profile of an old decayed Lord Byron. . . .

He was, I realise now, a cultivated spirit, infinitely superior to his children—to those mediocre champions of the church and army, to that idiot spinster, to that sullen and irascible widow. As a youth, he must have been sentimental and romantic, the intellectual of his times, nurtured on Byron and Lamartine, Alfieri and Aleardi. . . . I remember certain discussions he had with his children, and have engraved in my memory his words, exactly how he spoke them.

". . . I tell you once again—Alfieri should be praised for one thing at least: he found Italy Metastasiesque[1] and left it Alfieriesque!"

I can still see his upraised hand—a hand that was pale and of great nobility, the index finger adorned with a large cameo—and his beautiful head with its white hair shining in an oblique ray of sunshine—his wilful lips, his youthful blue eyes beneath the vast arch of his eyebrows.

But I never thought that he had had an austere life, or was a man of unbridled virtue. . . . He must have had a joyous existence . . . travelling much, loving many, squandering a great deal—according to the dictates of the poetry of his time. And his youth must have been adventurous, magnificent, as incredible as one of Chateaubriand's novels.

At the time of which I am speaking, this poor old man then lived for the most part at the expense of his daughter and the sunset of his life was not serene. This was obvious when the uncle-priest and uncle-captain were not there, and we were the only ones at table—the idiot and us children on one side, he and his daughter on the other.

She would provoke the count with that ruthless malevolent coldness that feels forced to bestow itself, knowing

---

1 A reference to Pietro Antonio Domenico Trapassi, who wrote under the pseudonym of Metastasio.

itself to be needed by the victim, and rarely would they get to the fruit course without a dispute—courtly and composed of eloquent silences mixed with a few bloody words. The usual arguments: a jewel to be given back, a horse to be bought, a bill to be paid; his dissipations, his former prodigality, pride, folly added to her refrain . . .

We children would remain silent, our eyes on an antique majolica platter, intent on the landing of Ulysses or the desolation of Penelope amidst beans in tomato sauce.

"*Je ne payerai pas, voilà tout!*"[1] she would say; then, in a slow, hissing voice: "*Vieux fou!*"[2]

"*Tu as dit? . . . Tu as dit? . . .*"[3]

The count would jump up from the chair with all the muscles of his face contracted from the insult of his daughter.

"*Tu as dit? . . .*"

Without answering, she would slowly fold up her napkin, calmly and mercilessly rise from her chair, and disappear.

The count followed her with his clear gaze, for a few seconds staring at the door through which she had disappeared, before suddenly turning toward us, smiling, his voice merry, clapping his hands as if to shake off his torment and our silence.

"*Ah! Les gamins! Les gamins! Maintenant où allons-nous aujourd'hui?*"[4] To Superga? To the race track? Gianduia?"

---

1 "I won't pay, that's all!"
2 "Old fool!"
3 "What did you say? . . . What did you say? . . ."
4 "Ah! Children, children! Where shall we go today?"

And while we talked at length about what we should do, he would walk around the dining room, alternating puffs on a cigarette with sips of cognac. Removing a book from the bookcase, he read aloud the strophes of some poet, making broad gestures, humming to himself, he stared at the sky and at the ceiling, dreaming . . .

He had great sympathy for me, and gave me preference over his grandson.

Possibly that old dreamer perceived in me, a strange, agitated, curious child, the seeds of future literary consumption . . .

During our long walks through the city or among the hills we would assault him with questions and we pulled at his hands if he hesitated to respond, and I remember even now, with admiration, the profundity of his explanations, the poetic clarity with which he made the workings of a lightning conductor or telephone seem simple—the metamorphosis of a bug-beetle, the anatomy of a flower.

However, the *sancta sanctorum* of our curiosity was his rooms.

"*Chez monsieur le Comte!*"[1] the servants would say solicitously.

"*L'appartement du Grand-Papa!*"[2] my friend would say mysteriously, applying his index finger to his lips.

We had to traverse the whole house to get to his rooms. A large double door opened into his study, the

---

1 "The apartments of Monsieur le Comte!"
2 "Grandfather's room!"

room with the balcony in flower. The stern and elegant
atmosphere revealed a dreamer, a person of refined sen-
sibilities, a scholar and a man of the world. To one side,
a large bookcase, protected by a series of marble busts
which filled me with wonder, reached to the ceiling.

"*Monsieur le corate, est-ce que c'est la tante Erneste, celle-
là?*"[1]

"*Ah! Non, mon petit,*" he said laughing, "*c'est Dante
Alighieri, le père des poètes.*"[2]

"*Alors, est-ce que c'est vous, monsieur le comte, ce
monsieur-là?*"[3]

"*Mais non! C'est Lord Byron, mon très-cher poète
anglais.*"[4]

Then he would pick up a huge illustrated *Divine
Comedy* from the bookshelves, or *Don Giovanni*, or *Il
Corsaro*, and we would flip through the beautiful prints
that were protected by sheets of tissue paper. Those were
hours of blissful dreams for me.

But my friend would get bored almost immediately and force his grandfather to do something more
cheerful.

So, the old man would play a harmonium on which
fountains spurted their spurting spiral-shaped glass and
shepherds and shepherdesses danced to a plaintive and
hoarse air. . . . Or we would go into the next room,
among the rarities that the Count had brought back from

---

1 "Monsieur le Comte, is that Aunt Erneste?"
2 "Ah! No, my little one," he said laughing, "that is Dante Alighieri,
the father of poets."
3 "So then is that gentleman there you, Monsieur le Comte?"
4 "But no! It is Lord Byron, my favourite English poet."

his Oriental travels, or he would drive our curiosity until we got to his bedroom which was decorated with Empire style wallpaper with yellow and turquoise stripes.

Finally we would come to the closed door, the mysterious room that no one had ever entered.

※

The closed room!

My friend talked to me about it often, while reading the tale of Bluebeard. . .

"*Tu sais que grand-papa aussi a une chambre où personne n'entre jamais. . . . Mini pas même,*" (and this said a lot!) "*ni les oncles, ni maman. . . . C'est défendu . . .*"[1]

"*Mais qu'est-ce qu'il y a donc au dedans?*"[2]

"*Sais pas . . . sais pas . . .*"[3] my friend would say, pulling in his shoulders with a mysterious terror.

My imagination lit up.

In the kitchen we tormented the servants for hours and hours.

"Mini, what's in there?"

"The prisoners of '48!" he would reply with a smile.

"It isn't true!"

"The savages of Malabar!" and he would smile again.

"It isn't true! Mini, you know but don't want to tell!"

He knew and didn't want to tell. He would let himself be assaulted—us jumping on his shoulders, grabbing his

---

1 "Do you know that grandfather has a room where nobody can enter? Not even Mini," (and this said a lot!) "not even the uncles or mother. . . . It's forbidden . . ."

2 "But what's in the room?"

3 "I don't know . . . I don't know."

knees, tearing at his red whiskers, beating him, but he would remain silent, smiling.

The cook intervened.

"Be good, little gentlemen! Calm down and I will tell you, in secret."

We let our victim go, deceived for a few seconds by this promise.

"The Count keeps a big beast in there, that he brought back from India, many years ago. . . . But only Mini is allowed to see it, and he goes to visit it twice a week."

We listened, not terribly convinced.

But meanwhile I thought of a good many other possibilities.

I have never been innocent.

I—who have always been and will always be incurably naïve—cannot find, going back even to my childhood, that thing called innocence, instead finding only my precocious self, my prepubescent malice, on the watch.

One day, while Mini and Ghita were tiring themselves out describing to us the imprisoned beast, with its fur and horns, tusks and tail, I interrupted those zoological marvels with the following conclusion:

"Vittorino! *J'ai compris maintenant ce qu'il y a au dedans! Il y a la bien-aimée de ton grand-papa!*"[1]

The two startled servants fell silent, looking at each other, letting themselves shrink into their chairs, desolated!

✳

---

1 "Vittorino! Now I know what is kept in there! It is your grandfather's lover!"

But the secret of the impenetrable room was not a *bien-aimée*, not a woman.

When I managed to reach the door—a huge seventeenth-century affair, inlaid with walnut and with brass knobs—I felt the wood and metal, listening anxiously to the noises on the other side.

Nothing, always nothing.

It was not a mystery of life or a mystery of death or of the past that was guarded in there—there were no women, but behind the heavy door pure spirits were imprisoned.

My imagination lost its way, I was tortured by curiosity.

I tortured my friend, who was already well accustomed that mystery, resigned to that prohibition—forcing him to set aside his games in order to spend hours on end with me in his grandfather's room, in order to lose ourselves in contemplation of the giant mysterious door, black and studded.

We would knock on grandfather's study door, and he would appear, smiling. But sometimes he would not answer. And so then we would cautiously open the door: the room was dark, the old man was not there. We would step back, turn, run away, frightened.

But one evening I took Vittorino by the hand and led him inside that gloomy darkness.

"*Il doit être dans la chambre de la bête farouche! Allons-nous la voir, allons-nous l'épier!*"[1]

---

1 "He must be in the room of the wild beast! Let's go and see it, let's go and spy on it."

"Non! Non! J'ai peur!"[1]

"Viens donc, lâche! Viens!"[2]

I pulled him through the dark rooms, us groping our way, through the study and the oriental room, into the bedroom.

The Count was in the mysterious room!

A band of light came from under the closed door, propagating itself over the shiny mosaic floor . . .

Kneeling down, without breathing, with our eyes fixed on the crack beneath the door, we tried in vain to see something; but the only thing that came to us was some odorous smoke, the smell of incense.

Blood was pulsing through my head with the violence of a mallet. In the silence I could hear my tiny heart beating, going in time with the gnawing of a wood-worm, with the tick-tock of the big pendulum-clock. Then a voice, the voice of the Count, indistinct, altered, in the same manner as when he recited poetry to us, but more urgent, first gasping in supplication, then pleading, almost as if doing so to more than one person, almost as if waiting in vain for a reply. . . . Amidst long pauses of sepulchral silence.

I didn't understand his words.

". . . horrible . . . pas plus . . . chevelure . . . épouse . . . Katty . . . Hortensia . . . souvenir . . . pardonner . . ."[3]

A long silence. Then a slow and heart-rending sigh, a sigh of desperate regret. Then a breath, and another

---

1 "No, no, I'm scared!"

2 "Come on coward, let's go!"

3 ". . . horrible . . . no longer . . . hair . . . spouse . . . bride . . . Katty . . . Hortensia . . . memory . . . forgive me . . ."

breath . . . the band of light was fading—the Count was blowing out the candles, about to come out . . .

We jumped to our feet, fleeing as quickly and silently as rats, taking refuge in the kitchen . . .

But an hour later we went back and knocked on the door of the old man's study. He welcomed us kindly; as usual he showed us the prints, and the books on science and travel. And seeing, through the rooms, the huge closed door, I could not stop myself, and gathering all my courage, asked quietly:

"*Et là dedans, monsieur le comte, est'il vrai qu'il y a une bête terrible?*"[1]

He looked at me, put his hand on the back of my neck, smiling:

"*C'est Mini qui dit ça? . . . C'est vrai. . . . Une bête terrible vraiment. . . .*"[2] Then he fell silent, then seemed to whisper, as if to himself: "*Le regret, mon enfant! . . .*"[3]

The years separated me from my friend. I learned of his exile to Paris, with his mother, who remarried.

I read, not long after, about Count Fiorenzo's death.

My childhood vanished in time.

Almost twenty years went by, twenty years made up of the days that we call life. I forgot.

When I was standing in front of his destroyed home with my dear seventy-five-year-old friend, one of those

---

1 "And in that room, Monsieur le Comte, is it true that there is a horrible beast?"
2 "Did Mini tell you this ? . . . It's true. . . . A truly horrible beast. . . ."
3 "Regret, my child! . . ."

women I prefer because they have left behind them, in the infinite remoteness, people, times, and countries, and their conversation for me has always the mysterious fascination of a fable, I thought again of Count Fiorenzo.

With a quick-witted intelligence, a *bon mot* always on her lips, she in the evenings would gather around her grey head all the suitors which she contested with pretty twenty-year-old geese. She was, however, a good, sentimental soul, who had seen a great deal, and who could understand, and pardon, everything. Possibly (there were a great many stories in circulation about her remote youth)—possibly that all might also be forgiven.

Noon was approaching. We went into a café.

"Thank you, dear. Treat me to a bitter, and a pastry for Khy-San."

We sat away from others, near a large window that looked out onto a busy street, me with the Japanese dog, a marvel of grace and ugliness, on my lap.

I looked out the window, past the new houses, at a large area of demolished neighbourhoods; and in the desolate sadness of these ruins, of the poles, the fences, I suddenly recognised the home of my childhood friend, already half destroyed, making out the entrance columns, and the big central balcony.

"Signora, did you ever know Count X?"

She made a gesture with both hands, and smiled broadly.

"And how! The Countess was one of my dearest friends. . . . An adorable creature! She was Maria Cristina's lady-in-waiting. She died of consumption, at a very young age. The Queen cried for her as if she had been a sister."

"And Count Fiorenzo . . ."

The lady stopped smiling.

She took Khy-San, who was whining, from my lap, and set him on hers, and in an altered voice murmured:

"*L'homme aux cinq cents maitresses . . .*"[1]

"Five hundred!"

"If not that many, a great many all the same. . . . Many of whom I also knew . . ."

And, remembering, she began to recite a few names, and with each name, the ghost of a woman who had long ago turned to dust appeared to my imagination.

"When did you meet him?"

"Eighteen years ago, signora. I was a friend of his grandson's."

"You should have seen him in his day! He had a freshness composed of perfect lines, strength, nobility, pride, and intelligence. . . . Women lost their reason over him. . . . But he was a man of refined sentiments, who had no love for the society of your era. . . . I have read your books and feel pity for you. Maybe I am old and can no longer understand such things, but these days, what is called love seems to me nothing but worldly gossip, an exchange of egoism and vanity . . ."

"Signora!"

"So it is, so it is . . ."

She stopped talking, taken by a fit of coughing and then breathlessness. With a trembling hand she straightened the silk ribbon that was tied behind the ears of Khy-San.

---

1 "The man of five hundred mistresses . . ."

"I was a child, but can remember that the last years of the Count were sad. His daughter . . ."

"A viper! For many years I did not visit that house because of her. The poor Count! . . . . It was from the loyal Mini, who I saw from time to time, that I got my news. . . . He was a dear fellow!"

And she let out a slow sigh which was reminiscent of another sigh, heartrending, heard who knows when or where, which had been asleep in me for years. . . . A memory suddenly flashed through my mind.

"Signora, do you recall having heard, among the Count's eccentricities, of a certain mysterious room?"

"So you know about this as well! It was a popular tale. The closed room!"

"But what was in it?"

"If I told you, you would laugh. And you would be wrong to. It would be better if you took that delicate man as an example.

"Old, decayed, exhausted, he had kept the poetry of his spring intact, had made a refuge where his decrepit heart could rejuvenate. He had collected, in that room, all the remains of the women he had loved. The *chambre à souvenirs* . . .

"Strange things were talked of.

"The walls were taken up by large closets. In the middle of the room stood a prie-dieu, with many little candles, many flowers. When the Count felt regrets, he closed himself in there, lighted all the candelabrum, burned incense, so that the air became sacred, as in a temple.

"He visited the closets, took things out, touched, kissed his memories one by one—the bridal dress and dried up orange blossoms of his dead bride, the bracelets and veil of a Persian woman, the lock of marvellous golden hair that Katty N. had cut and sent to him as a gift before killing herself with a knife in a hotel in Vienna . . . the rosary and wimple of a Carmelite nun, the enormous muff of one of Empress Eugenia's ladies-in-waiting, the gem-encrusted babouche of a famous courtesan who had acquired for him the King's protection—dresses, gloves, ribbons, belts, artificial flowers, dried flowers, all the most diverse and strange objects that a woman can leave behind; and portraits and portraits and letters and letters; and everything neatly arranged and catalogued, with a card on which was written a name and date . . ."

"A mad collector!"

"Maybe . . . but also a great poet! When he had looked through the closets, he would kneel down in front of them, at the luminous, flower-decked altar, and with his face in his hands he would call all the women of his youth by name. . . . For each of them he had composed a recalling strophe and all of them met there among the flowers, the candles, the incense—no longer rivals, no longer jealous, having become sisters in no longer being . . . or in being old women, which is the same thing, my dear Guido!"

Khy-San whined impatiently.

I looked, through the window, at the ruins of the far away house, at the entrance columns, at the balcony which was no longer in bloom. I thought of the old man,

kneeling down and officiating. . . . The demon of irony
insisted that I smile . . .

My friend looked at me with sadness.

"Don't laugh, don't laugh!"

She petted Khy-San, and quieted her with a cream-
pastry. There was in her voice and eyes a desperate regret,
which for me was an unquestionable revelation:

"You young people cannot understand. But it was
sweet to love, and sweet to be loved that way!"

A Spiteful Day

"YOU SEE, melancholy, in itself, is not considered by modern psychiatrists to be a mental illness but rather a basic symptom of manic-depressive disorders. Basic melancholy is characterised by the slowing down of the psychomotor process and thus by the slowing down of actions, and the fatigue that this brings about, so that the subject is assailed by a general sense of impotency, which beats them down, putting them in a gloomy state of mind. As for delusional melancholy, added to these phenomena are delirious ideas, particularly kinaesthetic delusions of emptiness. . . . In anxious or agitated melancholy, there are hypochondriacal ideas of negation, littleness, and self-reproach; the patient believes they are being persecuted, their interests ruined, their affections betrayed, and they hate others without reason. Finally, in dazed melancholy, the difficulty in motor expressions determines dazed conditions. But, are you listening?"

No, I am not listening to my friend. I let his arm drag me through the whirling of the crepuscular city, while with vacant eyes I gaze before me. I don't understand his words, only hearing his voice—his voice which is almost gay and which irritates me as if it were poking fun at my sickness.

I stare at the young doctor; he is talking with his face in profile, with a serene expression, his eyes lit up with the love for his science; and his serenity and faith fill me with anger. I would like to make him miserable. I free my arm from his, move away from him, and interrupt his speech:

"Would you mind not pontificating in such a loud voice? The passers-by are laughing at you. . . . Look!"

No one is laughing. This was just a pretext in order to tell him something unpleasant. There is so much cruelty in my voice that he pauses, looking at me thoughtfully:

"How perverse you are today! I haven't done you the slightest wrong!"

The afflicted voice of my good-hearted friend (yes, he is so much kinder, simpler and more straightforward!) does not move me. The fact that I'm conscious of being in the wrong is exasperating, forcing me to carry on with my cruel words. We walk for a while in silence, then I attempt another pretext to harm him, and putting on a calm and distracted voice ask:

"But, do you really believe in medicine?"

"What a question! As much as you do in poetry . . ."

"But I don't believe in poetry!"

And I laugh loudly.

"Oh, no! My heavens!" And my friend shakes my arm and talks to me with the child-like emphasis that he has managed to keep intact while concentrating on books and work in the laboratory. He talks to me about the Ideal, Science and Intimate Satisfaction.

"Intimate Satisfaction! I sincerely believe that you are joking! Or, if you are not joking, you are putting me on, or if you are not putting me on, you are a fool. My dear fellow, these days, the ideal is this: to exploit Science or Literature or Politics or any other nonsense in order to gain personal well-being as soon as possible, and to seize from the world our share of the prey . . ."

In order to hurt my naïve friend's feelings, I had lied. He no longer speaks. The sad expression on his face will last all evening. And this is what I wanted. We continue along the street, without destination, under the first light of the electric street lamps: my silent victim, with his head bowed, and me with a malicious smile on my lips, spying on the whirling crowd, on the lookout for another friend to bring down.

Why must we have, from time to time, these spiteful days in our lives?

It is an evil that comes along unexpectedly, without apparent cause. I don't have the slightest problem, morally or materially; the world has been indulgent towards me, life is good.

At breakfast, I ate, laughed and, saying all sorts of silly things, made my mother and brother laugh until they cried. I was happy and left the house early, in order to dive into the beautiful winter sun; walking over the better part of the Valentino,[1] alone with my carefree joy.

---

1 A park in Turin much frequented by Gozzano.

The virgin snow, crystallised by the cold, covered the park in dazzling, soft, wavy whiteness, on which was a sweet quality that went with the rhythm of my dreams. The clear sky contrasted with the silver of the earth, and the blackness of the naked trees, as if engraved in pure turquoise.

I recited a few verses out loud and then whistled a Tannhäuser motif. I sunk my hand into the compact snow, made a snowball which I nibbled on to wet my throat, with the delight of a schoolboy on holiday.

And, almost without realizing it, I came up directly behind two elderly men who had been walking in front of me for some time.

Then something happened, insignificant, almost comic, unconfessable, which at a blow darkened my every joy.

The older of the two took out an onyx, gold-trimmed snuffbox; he took a pinch, sniffed it, and offered the box to his companion with a slow, trembling gesture. And since the pathway narrowed between two piles of snow, it was necessary for me to remain behind them, and suddenly I was assailed by the terrible smell of a *Cerambyx moschatus*,[1] which I could see on the bottom of the open snuffbox, amidst the reddish dust—the blue elytrons, the long curved antennae of the insect I loathe. There is nothing else that has the power to make me mortally sad so much as the odour of this innocent coleopteron.

Subtle bonds connect it to remote things of my childhood: an old primary school teacher I had, a hollow willow

---

1 The musk beetle—so-called for its smell.

tree in the cemetery, and other memories—indefinable, inexpressible in words.

For a few seconds I had to breathe in its detestable aroma and, by the time I managed to overtake the two old men, my soul had already been poisoned. My joy was no longer with me; and that silver carpet and turquoise sky make me rejoice no more. Melancholy had come up beside me with his silent steps, squeezing my heart with the cruel nails of his bony hands.

I am desperate.

In the world, there are men who die from cold and hunger, men oppressed by the saddest moral misfortunes, by the most terrible physical illnesses; but I feel that no one is more unhappy than I, that no one could suffer more.

It is not the sentimental, long-desired and almost sweet melancholy of my adolescence; it is darkness, the emptiness of a man falling into a bottomless abyss. The town disappears; the light disappears, and science and all other things that make life worth living. The soul is desperate, already damned and without hope, swept away by the endless fury of the pit of hell.

Ah, to be no more! If only a simple act of willpower would suffice to abolish us, to take us back to the way we were before we were! A disdainful bitterness against myself, against my fellow men, pierces my heart, embittering my blood like those steel blades that turn the juice of the sweetest fruits bitter and corrupt.

A perverse desire has taken hold of me, a need to make others suffer as I do. I made my doctor friend miserable. He follows me in silence. And now I search in the crowd, on the lookout for a new victim.

There's one. Quinteri. I did not recognise him at first. He is wearing a new overcoat—an English overcoat that he has been expecting for three weeks. I walk behind him for a spell. He certainly is the most elegant of my friends—an arbiter of taste and the herald of the slightest shades of line and colour. And I know just how to wound him.

I'm just near him; he turns towards me, smiling:

"Oh! My dear fellow, how are you?"

"Not bad. I only just recognised you . . ."

Quinteri stops walking, turning his body around in exultation.

"What do you think?"

"I mistook you for a barber on holiday."

"Are you joking?"

"Not really. . . . I am not very fond of the colour and the cut of the shoulders."

He becomes pale; he stammers, trembling as if he is being obliged to defend his honour against some atrocious calumny.

"Speak! You can at least explain yourself! The colour? Does it seem too lively? The Duke of Abruzzi has one exactly like it."

"The Duke of Abruzzi is a hero; but he has never been a very elegant fellow."

"And the shoulders? What's wrong with the shoulders?"

"A false line."

"False? But it is as refined as possible! You do realise that the current fashion is to have the shoulders at once abundant and fragile, so they don't fit quite right, giving the overcoat a hint of being someone else's."

"But this one gives the impression of being a mediocre overcoat that is absolutely your own."

Quinteri attempts to give an explanation, to defend himself again; but the man has been beaten, mortally wounded in what he holds most dear.

"Are you two arguing?"

Unexpectedly Tibaldi comes up between us, his voice happy, and we walk on.

"No, we were just discussing a few trifles. . . . But, Tibaldi, you have put on cologne!"

"I'm going to Her house for dinner!" (Her is his fiancée). "It's the middle of April. I am happy my friends! You have my permission to be envious!"

"I don't envy you. You are going through a very natural physiological period. You are in love. The thing you believe to be a divine intoxication, an experience unique in this world, is a phase that is both illusory and temporary."

Tibaldi makes a gesture of silent protest.

"It is not to upset you that I say this," I continue. "You are blind, and deaf—all your senses dull. The grouse, the cleverest of all the wildfowl, during its mating season, becomes so silly that it lets hunters catch it with their bare hands. We will see each other in a few months, when the fog of your honeymoon will have faded away and the first unadmitted bitterness sprung up inside of you—the first inevitable disappointments. But of course—it would be nice to think that you will have *a very happy marriage!*"

Tibaldi makes a gesture of angry protest.

"Enough already! Now, have the courtesy to admire, in silence!"

And he takes out a medallion that he wears near his heart, with a photo of her on it, and we pass it amongst ourselves, in a chorus of praises and flattering words.

"Beautiful!"

"Exquisite!"

"The beautiful Simonetta!"

"The famous Miss Borelli!"

"She is beautiful, my dear Tibaldi, truly beautiful. *Tibi gratulor!*[1] And I pretend to contemplate the image in rapture. "I'm squinting a little—it's a little game I like to play with my imagination. Whenever I have a photo of a beautiful woman in front of me, I amuse myself by making her thirty or forty years older. At this precise moment, I see the face of your fiancée—at nearly seventy years old. Add a triple chin to the oval of her jaw, draw three wrinkles on her forehead, a few more around her eyes, lips and nose; replace the bright, natural wave of her hair with a thick, frizzy black wig . . ."

Tibaldi grabs the medallion from my hands and puts it back near his heart.

"I warn you—you shall not be the man I have to write about my wedding!"

He smiles, but without his previous gaiety. His voice has changed; and this evening, in front of the blonde

---

1 Latin: "I congratulate you!"

eighteen-year-old girl, he will not be able to avoid think-ing for a few seconds of her future wrinkles, her future false hair.

Two more friends join the ranks of my victims: a lieu-tenant and a poet.

With loud laughter, I assault the poet.

"You seem to be in a very good mood! Why the laughter?"

"I am laughing because I see another poet."

And I deliver a long speech to my young and enthu-siastic friend, explaining how poetry is a bit of a sham. As for my military friend, who is a fervent nationalist—I attempt to demolish every bit of his faith, pursuing him with enormous blunders, parading my political and so-cial ignorance before him. And the awareness that I am in the wrong, the awareness that I am abusing the goodness of my all too patient friends, exasperates me more and more.

"But you don't seem well! Look at yourself, my poor friend!"

I see myself reflected in a large shop window. I am green.

Without hardly saying goodbye, I leave my friends, and make my way home. Once there, I immediately take refuge in my study, under the influence of that precau-tionary instinct that hydrophobics have when they are near their loved ones. Nobody will see me this evening. I don't want to make my mother and my brother, the people I love, miserable.

On my writing desk I find something that, of a sud-den, makes me feel better. A picture postcard—a greeting from an alpine guide, showing a landscape of evergreens and snowfields, which is sweet to my memory.

As if by magic, I feel better. My spiteful sadness has disappeared. An innocent beetle brought it about, a simple picture postcard with greetings from a mountain climber has made it completely vanish.

I feel better. This spiteful sickness, which for so many hours turned my soul evil, will not return for weeks, for months.

I am well again. Smiling, laughing.

I stand up and gaze at a large print by Albrecht Dürer: *Melencolia I,* which presides over my hours of work and meditation.

The great earthly angel with eagle's wings, the sleepless spirit, sits on a bare rock, with his elbow on his knee, his cheek supported by his fist, a book resting on his other leg and a compass in his other hand. At his feet, curled up like a serpent, lies a loyal greyhound, the dog that has hunted in the company of men since before the dawn of time.

Nearby, perched on the edge of a millstone like a bird, an already sad boy sleeps, holding the stylus and tablet with which he must write the first word of his science. And, scattered about, are the various tools of human labour; and over his watchful head, near the top of his wing, the silent sands of Time glide through an hourglass.

And in the background one can see the ocean with its gulfs, harbours and lighthouses, calm and indomitable, over which, before the glory of a rainbow sunset, a vespertine bat flies, the revealing word inscribed on its wings. And those harbours and those lighthouses and those cities were built by this sleepless spirit, who is crowned with patience. He cut the stone for the towers, pulled down the pines for the ships, tempered the iron for every battle.

It was he who imposed on Time a device to measures it. And the great earthly angel with eagle's wings, on whose hips bound with steel hang the keys that open and close, answers those who question him in this way:

"The sun sets. The light that is born in Heaven, dies in Heaven; and the light of today ignores the light of tomorrow. But night is one; and its shadow sits on the faces of all. I know that the living are like the dead, the awake are like those who sleep, the young are like the old, since one changes to the other; and each change has pain and joy as equal companions. I know that the harmony of the universe is made of discord and that the high path is the same as that which is below. However, despite my knowledge, I continue to do my work, that is both manifest and occult. I see some have perished while I still last; I see others last on, eternally beautiful. I see that all things change in front of fire, like good before gold, and one thing alone is constant: my courage. I lie down, only to rise again!"

A Dream

LAST NIGHT Balbina Peyrot appeared to me once more.

At table everyone was indifferent when I told them about my dream.

In vain I tried, once again, to explain to my mother and brother that sweet and terrible thing. I talked at length, picking out the right words, before realizing, as usual, that they were coarse, without meaning, unable to express the mysterious, unknown, subconscious, and ineffable qualities of my vision. My brother no longer listened to me, and my mother, simply to be kind, pretended to be interested, interrupting me with a suggestion:

"You shouldn't work at night and it would be better to not eat those cherries with cognac . . ."

Alas! Not even to those nearest to us, to those who are always the most understanding, can the world of our dreams be explained in words.

Balbina Peyrot. She has been a familiar part of our family since time immemorial, not so much due to the little photograph of her hanging between those of my grandfather and my mother's uncle, but because she has been a fixed idea of mine, an obsession since my early years. As a child, I remember climbing on a chair in order to be face to face with the effigy of this lady and contemplate her for a long time, without talking, without batting an eyelash or smiling, with a pensive seriousness that made the maids laugh and worried my mother.

The mysterious charm which emanated from that somewhat exaggerated oval cannot be put into words—those lips holding a triangular smile, the oblong eyes with their overly large arching eyebrows, and that unruly lock of brown hair which was escaping from her yellow turban.

Later I would softy pronounce the name that was written in reddish ink on the back of the miniature: *Balbina Peyrot*; and in a different handwriting, with a faded pencil, was added: *actress*. Nothing else. And since then, I have dreamt about her as I do today, and will forever more—a vision at once tenacious and pure, sweet and terrible, that makes me weep in my dreams for that love that in real life I have never had—that makes me weep the tears in my dreams that, in real life, I no longer know how to shed.

The vision repeats itself, always exactly the same. One could say that it has been incised on my mind like an engraving on a steel plate, like a piece of music on a wax phonograph cylinder.

An invisible spirit presides over the vision, putting in motion the fine mechanism of my nerves, and the dream begins, exact, invariable, like the dizzying projection of a reel of film. Nothing indicates its coming.

I fall asleep in the evening, in my bed, without worries. And suddenly, my "I", with a mysterious shiver of anxiety, is startled to find that it is not asleep; the first and only thought of my waking conscience is this:

"You are going to dream!"

I try to stir myself, to wake myself up, with an impetus of mad rebellion against the martyrdom that awaits me.

It is a sort of wordless dialogue between my conscience and the spirit which incites the vision and accompanies me through the mystery.

The spirit is behind me, unknown, invisible; I can vaguely discern it, however, if I suddenly turn around; but it escapes, hiding itself behind my back. It is a shadow without shape or colour.

And it speaks to me without words. (Whoever is reading this should replace my dull words, the apathetic material of my description, with musical notes).

"You are going to dream . . ."

"No! No! I don't want to!"

"You are going to dream!"

"I don't want to! I want to wake up! I can still wake myself up!"

With all my strength I rebel in order to take back my life, to take myself back to reality. I open my eyes.

"See, I'm awake and safe!"

I'm awake, in the garden, sitting on the iron bench which encircles the hundred-year-old horse chestnut. The house is there before me, lit up by the June sun. I look at the sundial. It's three o'clock. I am not dreaming. One cannot see such minute details in a dream.

The garden flaunts all the harmony of the liveliest hues. The blue that surrounds the exquisitely green leaves of the horse chestnuts seems as if cut out of pure turquoise. I am not dreaming. A white Pieridea passes through a ray of sunlight, pauses, and then continues on. Trembling golden disks are laid out over the gravel, each pebble of which is neat, distinct, them now and again sparkling like crushed gems. . . . I'm saved! I'm no longer dreaming! . . .

"You are not dreaming? You think that you are not dreaming? You're fooling yourself! . . ."

"No, no, I am not dreaming! This is the garden, that is the house!"

"You are wrong! You are dreaming of not dreaming, you're dreaming of being where you are . . ."

The shadow keeps silent but I can feel it behind my back, motionless. It's true! I've been tricked! Here I am under its spell! There is no way out, I can't escape the martyrdom that awaits me! But the house is there; the windows are open, so I will call out, and someone will come to rescue me.

I try to get up, to scream . . .

Ah! The frightening martyrdom! My mouth is sealed by a heavy hand, my body is tied to the bench with a thousand ropes. I rebel, struggle, become tense, twisting and writhing . . .

I suffer the unspeakable.

And the house is there before me, lit up by the sun. The same butterfly as before flutters over the grass. The sky, through the leaves of the horse chestnut, is as if cut out of pure turquoise.

My eyes, dilated with anxiety, fix themselves on my brother's window. It is open. Why doesn't he show himself like he has so many times before? Why doesn't a woman come out into the garden? Why this silence? Ah! If only I could make myself heard!

The shadow is behind me, talking to me without words:

"Do you want to see your brother?"

"Yes, yes!" I sob, with sudden hope.

"Well, there he is!"

And at these words my brother appears at his window sill. From his profile, he seems preoccupied. In his shirtsleeves, he is cleaning his rifle. But why does he not look this way?

Ah, finally! He leaves off what he is doing and comes out onto the balcony, arms folded. Looking out over the garden, he stares at me. I move my head, imploring him with a desperate gaze. He stares at me for a long time, but doesn't see me; with a familiar gesture, he runs a hand through his hair, and then disappears.

Ah! The frightening martyrdom!

"Did you see?" the pitiless spirit asks. "In vain do you delude yourself that you can seek help from the living. Your voice cannot be heard by human beings. This beautiful sun is not that which shines on the Earth, but that which illuminates the kingdom of shadows. . . . You think you are in your garden, in front of your house—but you are alone with me, beyond time and space, in the kingdom of no longer being, of not yet being . . ."

"Enough! Enough already! Let me wake up or let me die!"

"Here, you are not able to die. . . . I know," the ruthless shadow continues. "I know why you are trembling so much. . . . I know who it is that terrifies you . . ."

"If you know, then have mercy!" I sob with fresh dread, since I understand what the spirit means, since I feel the time of atrocious martyrdom fast approaching.

A mad fury against the tormenting spirit possesses me. I try to turn around, to see it, to grab hold of it; I shout at it:

"Ah, curse you! Do as you will, torment me to the best of your ability! What do I care about your puerile game? With everything I see, I have this consoling certainty: I know that I am dreaming."

"So, you think you are dreaming? Fine, but I tell you that you are not."

"No, it isn't true, I'm dreaming!"

"I tell you that you are no longer dreaming!"

I am no longer dreaming. Ah! Finally! I've woken up! I'm no longer bound and can speak. I get up from the bench in which I have been kept prisoner and take a few steps over the gravel which crunches beneath my feet . . .

I am no longer dreaming. I've escaped from the cruel spirit. This time, I will not see her. Breathing a sigh of relief, I relax.

I look at my brother's window. I would like to go up and tell him about my horrible dream.

Calmly, I walk through the garden, enter the foyer, and come to the hallway.

And what I see is unspeakable.

The staircase is no longer there . . .

Am I dreaming? No, I am not. This is reality. I touch my hands and cheeks: it's me: awake, conscious, reasoning.

The staircase that leads to the rooms of my mother and brother are no longer there. The newer wing of the house is entirely gone. But in front of me is a vestibule that I don't recognise, with columns and arches, dark and frightening. In dismay I retreat, turning and running back out to the garden.

The garden has also changed: the hundred-year-old horse chestnuts and firs are no longer there, replaced by unknown trees, and the flowerbeds have a different aspect, a boxwood hedge pruned into rounded shapes runs along the lawn; situated in front of the house are a few orange trees in sculpted vases that I have never seen before.

I'm not dreaming. I am certain that I am not dreaming. This is the truth, the frightening truth! If only I were dreaming and could have the cruel spirit near me to assure me that I was dreaming! Now, I think of it as a saviour, a friend.

But instead, I am alone, alone with my madness. I run to the other side of the house. Through the open windows, I can see the dining room: I go in; it is almost unchanged; I recognise the panels above the doors, with their hunting scenes and fruit, the two decrepit cupboards—those familiar objects fill my heart with hope. I enter the room: it is almost unchanged. Only a few objects and some furniture worry me; the colours are fresher, the fabrics and the frames livelier. Coming in through the open windows is the light of that strange sun—a sun that shines on things so they speak, that illuminates the kingdom of shadows, of no longer being, of not yet being . . .

With nervous eyes I look for the photograph of Balbina Peyrot. It is not there.

And here I am, at the final torture. An unspeakable thing occurs, a phenomenon both inside and outside myself, which human words cannot explain.

I hear—with a sense which is not hearing—an indistinct noise, far away. I see—with a sense which is not sight—an indefinite shape which in a short while will be coming into the room and which I am afraid to see again. And I know, suddenly, that it is that same spirit, and feel that it will return in a visible form.

Added to my terror, is a lively curiosity, which keeps me there, frozen in the middle of the room, waiting.

The shadow is not far away.

My sixth sense—which is an amalgamation of sight, hearing and I don't know what other senses—allows me to see in the distance, through the wall, the soul that I am expecting.

It is Balbina Peyrot.

She comes to the gate, and opens it . . . walks across the courtyard, along the walkway . . . into the garden, where she stops . . . then into the foyer.

My heart leaps with joy; she is not coming to kill or harm me. But I am filled with a fresh anxiety. I have caused her pain and must acknowledge to her that unpardonable wrong. And so, wishing to run away, I rush toward the door that leads to my room, but it resists, even as I hold the handle, shaking it with both hands.

The shadow reaches the next room, crosses it, and is now on the threshold, behind me.

I turn around to defend myself and find myself face to face with Balbina.

The face that I fear so much is sweet, sweet and worn by sadness, not in profile, as in the miniature, but facing me, without the turban, her hair disarranged, as if after some struggle.

The martyrdom of my anxiety ceases and that of remorse begins—a remorse that originates from that poor face which is there in front of me, from those sad, calm, eyes which are fixed on me without anger, as if she had received some mortal blow that she was now pardoning.

With unspeakable effort, we lean toward each other, me wishing to cry out:

"Forgive me!"

And she, maybe, to tell me, "You are forgiven!"

But an unknown force, the Irreparable, hinders our gestures and our words.

Now I know that Balbina will soon disappear, that this is a dream that I don't want to be dreaming. I want to hold her, speak to her, and make her speak.

"Forgive me! Forgive me!"

An inhuman remorse tears at my heart and, gazing into those sad eyes, I begin to feel the trembling of a convulsive sob coming from my throat. Little by little, tears begin to line my face—slow, heavy, warm, like drops of blood—the tears that, in real life, I no longer know how to shed. Balbina's face fades; I want to hold her, and make a desperate effort to do so.

"Forgive me! Forgive me!"

Diaphanous as snow on water, the oval shape disappears, followed by her sad lips which yearn to speak—her eyes, the last survivors, still staring at me in a desperate farewell, before they dissolve into the Irreparable. Then, nothing more. And then I too become annihilated, finally finding peace in a dreamless torpor.

This is the vision that repeats itself, always exactly the same, though occasionally incomplete. Sometimes the prelude and the whole atrocious conversation with the invisible spirit are missing and the dream begins with the appearance of the stairway. And sometimes it is the last part that is missing and, when the shadow is standing behind me while I try to force the resisting door, I suddenly wake up and the dream is over.

Oftentimes, I am curious and hope that the vision will continue, so that I can know more about the shadow and our vicissitudes; but, complete or not, the dream is always the same in its particulars, without the smallest incident being added, like the events recorded on a reel of film.

Maybe the secret of this nightmare, the beginning and the end of this encounter, is outside myself, in brains that have been turned to dust for many years.

About Balbina Peyrot, I have never been able to get precise information.

The old people in the village don't know a thing. An eighty-year-old woman muttered some uncertain information to me, which her aunt, a family servant of ours from long ago, had told her.

It seems that Balbina Peyrot was a young actress who had spent a certain period in our house, as a guest of my great-uncle, on my mother's side of the family.

The dream repeats itself all too often, leaving me prostrate, unable to work.

"Doctors of the soul" have been consulted but they can only suggest baths and opiates. But the origin of this evil is not in my brain, just as the inhuman remorse that is tearing at me for a crime I did not commit does not come from within myself.

It is in other people who are no longer here.

Maybe in my great-uncle with the large cravat, to the right side of Balbina.

Because those who smile down from the paintings and photographs, did not leave us heirs to their blood alone, but also their spirit—those enviable firstborn who sleep a dreamless sleep, and wake no more.

The Soul of the Instrument

IN the distant past, when the violin had not yet been invented, there lived in the forests of Bohemia a beautiful girl by the name of Rekma. Her family lived in a pine log cabin, the roof of which was covered with lichen and moss. The mother and daughter sewed the family's leather clothing and cooked meat; the father and four sons left each morning with heavy axes on their shoulders to go about their daily labour.

They were happy and Rekma was much loved. When her father spoke to her he softened the sound of his gruff voice. The colossal, hairy, gloomy brothers tamed themselves to become like shy children before her fragile, lily-like grace. With axes in hand they confronted terrible bears in order to offer her their soft furs; they searched amongst the rocks for rare, brightly-coloured gemstones to make magnificent barbarian necklaces for her.

And Rekma was happy.

From the clearing where the cabin was built, Rekma could see, on top of a bleak mountain, the grey walls of an ancient castle. It had been uninhabited for years. Strange legends were told about that deserted manor and the woodsmen avoided passing under the shadow of its towers at night.

One day the girl saw a very large banner made of scarlet silk waving from its merlons; the descendant of the old lords had returned to his paternal castle. The forest, which for long had only rung with the blows of the axe, now echoed with the sound of horns, the cries of hunters, and the yelping of hounds.

It was autumn and Rekma was walking through the woods when, all of a sudden, she heard the gallop of a horse and hid among the trees. Through the yellowing leaves she saw a knight dressed in silver riding a white horse that was caparisoned in green.

He swept by the girl like a whirlwind, his cape and the feathers on his hat whipping in the wind, his silver trumpet knocking against his saddle. With wide eyes Rekma followed that magnificent vision as it became lost in the forest. From that day on, she was no longer at peace. Often she saw the silver knight chasing deer and wild boar, furtively spying on him from amongst the bushes and rocks.

One evening when, tired from the hunt, he was returning home, reins abandoned on his horse's neck, Rekma dared to offer him a cluster of fat, shiny blackberries. He took them, without bothering to so much as glance at her. This arrogance made the girl's love grow stronger.

Taken by a limitless desperation, she would wander like a madwoman along the forest paths, lingering in the evening in the wildest places.

And one evening she found herself alone in a forlorn, frightening spot; the earth was blackened from old coal pits; through the trunks of thousand-year-old oaks, the howling of dogs came to her; on the horizon was the thin and bloody arc of the crescent moon. The time and place were right for enchantments. Rekma wanted to invoke the help of an evil spirit. And a spirit appeared.

"What is it you want of me?"

"I love a man who does not love me," the young woman murmured.

"I might be able to incline his feelings toward you . . ."

"You *might* be able to?"

"I could. But I won't do something for nothing . . ."

Rekma had heard about horrible pacts made with the Enemy. She shivered.

"What is it you ask for your services?"

"Oh, nothing much! Only your father."

"My father?" the girl cried. "Never!"

The Enemy stamped his cloven hoof on the ground and disappeared.

Long days of wretched passion went by. One morning Rekma saw the silver knight riding along, more handsome, more disdainful than ever. She leaned against a trunk, her heart leaping in her chest. And before her the shadow of the evil spirit appeared.

"If you wanted, you could be his wife within the hour."

"His wife?"

"Yes, if you abandon your father to me."

"Then take him!" Rekma cried out desperately.

And so the evil spirit dragged her to a crossroads in the forest where the woodsman was at work. Rekma's heart shrunk when she saw her beloved father in the hands of the Enemy, by her own fault. She wanted to scream, to defend him, but some unknown force paralysed both her voice and movement. The Enemy sunk its claws into the man's shoulders and twirled him dizzyingly around his head like a sling. When he stopped, the human form had disappeared, and between the fingers of the evil spirit there was now a sort of box, flat and solid and furnished with a curved handle.

"And now," the Enemy said, "give me your brothers; the instrument that has to seduce the Prince is not yet complete."

"My brothers?" Rekma cried, thrusting her hands through her hair in horror. "No! Never!"

Gloomily, she returned to the cabin. On the edge of the meadow, in the shadow of the oaks, her four brothers were sleeping, tired from their work. Rekma sat near them, placing her head in her hands. From the direction of the castle, at intervals, came the echo of horns and trumpets. And then the hunt got closer. Through the dark foliage of the pines she saw once again the handsome prince . . .

Her spouse?

"His bride," murmured the Enemy with fervent breath, appearing next to her. "Give me your brothers!"

Rekma loved her brothers; but madness clouded her mind. She covered her eyes with one hand and with the other made a desperate gesture of acceptance.

The evil spirit grabbed the index finger of the eldest brother in his left hand. The tip of the finger stuck out from his closed fist and, with his free hand, he pinched it and began to pull it like a thread through the eye of a needle. When Rekma uncovered her eyes, she saw half of her brother's body squished against the bottom of the diabolical fist and the other half coming out of the top in the form of a long, thin steel wire.

Standing more motionless than the indifferent trees, she saw what was left of her brother gradually decrease as it passed through the evil fist, the wire at the same time becoming longer and thinner. When his entire body had been transformed into wire, the Enemy cut off a piece, the length of an arm.

"This much should do. Let's move on to the next."

The second eldest was sleeping with one arm locked around the trunk of a fir. The Enemy grabbed him by the feet and, twisting him rapidly as a rope-maker does when making a rope, stepping back a little at a time, spun a thread that continued to grow longer and thinner until the youth's body disappeared like hemp on a distaff.

Once the rope had become thin and shiny, the evil spirit cut a piece the same length as the first. He then went to the third brother and, grabbing him by the head and feet, jumped on his body, kneading it with his cloven hoofs, in the same manner a baker does dough; and the youthful body lost its shape, becoming malleable, transparent, luminous like glass. The Enemy drew out a long sparkling thread and cut a piece off the same length as the others.

Only the youngest brother was left. Rekma cried out, but her voice was without sound as in a dream; then she rushed to the adored youth to protect him, to save him; she lifted him in her arms, but her legs would not let her run away.

"Marvellous!" said the Enemy, and grabbed a hair from youth's blond beard and began to quickly pull on it, while Rekma cradled her brother in her arms with the same regular motion that she had used when helping her mother to unravel a skein.

And the weight of the youth, little by little, grew less, and before long she let her useless arms fall to the ground; the fourth-born had entirely turned into a blond ball of string that the Enemy was bouncing viciously in his hands.

He cut a piece the same length as the rest. Rekma's four brothers were no more. To the curved handle of the flat and sonorous box that had been the body of the woodsman, the Enemy attached the four strings: one that was rather thick, the next somewhat thinner, then one thinner still, and the fourth extremely thin.

Rekma grabbed the instrument.

"Wait," the evil spirit told her quietly, "it is not yet finished."

"What more do you want from me, you cursed being?" Rekma cried.

"Not much. . . . Just that which is left."

Rekma lowered her head in agitation. She loved her mother more than her father, more than her brothers, more than anything.

"My life instead! Ask me for my life!"

"Your life? No, it's your soul that I want . . ."

The Enemy disappeared into the forest, making the strings of the violin vibrate as he went, and in that receding melody Rekma thought she could hear her brothers' voices. Dull night descended on the tops of the ancient oaks.

Rekma went to the cabin, pausing at the door without being seen, to contemplate her mother who sat near the fire, her chin resting in her hands, her beautiful silver hair lit up by the flashes of the fire. Rekma wanted to go inside and throw herself in her arms, to rescue her and be rescued, but the evil spirit stroked her with his eager words.

"Think about what you are doing . . . or everything will be lost!"

Rekma could no longer see anything. In a low voice, a voice so low that no one but the tempter could hear, she agreed, and then hid her face in her apron.

"Don't be frightened. It's already been done."

Rekma looked. Her mother's body was now nothing more than a flexible stick, the silver hair of the vanished woman protruding from one end. The evil spirit pulled and fastened the hair to the other end and created a bow. He ran it over the four stretched strings, turned the keys to tune the instrument, and began to play. And in the music Rekma could make out the dull rhythm of four axes as they moaned: "What have you done to your brothers?"

She grabbed the enchanted instrument and ran away.

✳

Reaching the castle walls and obeying the tempter's instructions, she began to circle around them playing the bewitched instrument.

The Prince was lying down in the royal bedroom, extremely pale, having been wounded on the hip by a wild boar during the last hunt. Suddenly he became aware of the charming music and sat up on the damask blankets to listen.

Rekma had circled the castle once. The Prince no longer felt the pain of his wound, which had healed as if by magic and, while the girl was making her second round, playing as she went, he dressed himself, putting on all his beautiful jewels, silks, and velvets, and thus adorned with these fabulous riches, felt sad at being so poor.

The music, passing once more beneath his windows, became so tragic that the Prince put a hand to his heart.

"I no longer feel the pain of my wound, but feel that my heart will always suffer if I don't find she who is calling me . . ."

He went down the stairs, dashed across the drawbridge, and fell to his knees at Rekma's feet, pressing his hands to that heart of his, which was being broken by the music.

Rekma stared at him, smiling bitterly:

"Ah! Why did you need to hear this music to be attracted to me?"

"I don't know! Your melody transports me, holds and conquers me like a choir of human voices telling me that you are the bride chosen for me by destiny . . ."

In her happiness, Rekma forgot about all else.

The marriage was celebrated with a magnificence that would never be seen again and the daughter of the woodsman became the princess of the magnificent castle.

But after some time the Prince was taken by vague worries, dull melancholy, even the love he had for his bride seeming to fade. Rekma would then take the violin and play, and the Prince's passion would be ignited anew.

On the day of the first anniversary of their marriage, while the husband and wife were sitting at the dining table, a stranger wrapped to his neck in a vermillion mantle entered. Rekma, recognizing his cloven hooves, let out a scream and ran to find refuge next to her husband. But the evil spirit set his claws into them both and carried them away in his desperate embrace, as if they were pieces of straw.

The magic instrument was left in the abandoned castle. One day a gypsy who was by chance passing through the ruins found it in a bronze case and picked it up. He began playing it, entranced and stunned by that instrument that screamed, implored, laughed and cried with a human voice. He made his way down to the lowlands, walking through the villages playing—men, women and children abandoning their work and games, to follow him, enchanted.

And he, at will, could make them laugh and cry.

After a Tragic Vow

"MY LUGGAGE! My luggage!"

Lost! The nine zinc trunks on which I had, with my very own hand, painted the tricoloured flag in order to recognise them in the chaos of the train stations and ports, were lost. I had lost the skins of the tiger, the panther, the python, and the birds of paradise skins—eight hundred birds of paradise from New Guinea: a fortune! And the cases and the jars of rare insects. All the treasures of a year's worth of hard work and exile: lost!

Ah! The Lambahadam train station, buried under the green of the coconut trees in the far south of Hindustan! I thought I was going crazy. And having to explain myself, haggle and fret in a foreign language with a native station master—a Christ made of bronze and dressed in a braided uniform, who was trying to console me by citing another case in which other precious luggage had been lost in that network of telegraphic lines that spreads out over the entire peninsula—a peninsula thirty times the size of Italy—like a net.

"Curse the hour that I decided to return to my country by train, travelling across the whole of Hindustan! At this moment I should be floating on the cerulean calmness of the Indian Ocean, sitting on a deck-chair, with a cigarette between my lips, and the latest mischief by Weber[1] in my hands, waiting for the breakfast bell to sound—my boxes resting, well taken care of, in the hold of the ship. Damned it!"

My travelling companion, a Frenchman, a consular agent who I had met in Madura, didn't dare to cheer me up with jokes anymore, repeating mechanically: "*C'est rigolo, c'est rigolo . . .*"[2] But anyhow, along comes the boy who was sent to the Post Office to collect our telegrams; he is bringing us the mail: letters and newspapers that have bounced along through twenty stations: unpleasant news from Italy; a letter from my mother who is being tormented by the abuses of an old great-uncle, a priest from Genoa, a nuisance and a torment in our family from time immemorial; and three issues of an important Italian literary review. I open one and read the most poisonous name I know: Tita Vinadio, signed beneath twenty pages about my latest book—which I wrote with all the love and sacrifice of six years of my youth—certainly saying things that will be of little pleasure to me. But no, it can't be possible! It's not a review: it's a series of comical insults, of witticisms à la *Guerrin Meschino*,[3] of personal inquiries, written in a style which is like a collaboration between a public clerk and a peevish spinster schoolmistress. And this inside the most important magazine, the official organ of Italian Literature!

---

1 Probably Albrecht Weber, the German Indologist and historian.
2 "How funny, how funny . . ."
3 An Italian chivalric romance written by Andrea da Barberino in 1410.

Back home, this sort of delight would cause five minutes of bad humour and nothing more. But, over here, deep in idolatrous India! In the Refreshment Room of a barbarian station, with my soul shattered by a mortal anxiety, it gives me nausea and an unjustified spite towards my homeland and evokes the figure of that Roman literator, blond as a German, petulant, loquacious, shrill, a strange double of Camillo di Cavour as depicted in the caricatures by Teja.[1]

I aggressively rise from my seat. How strange! I am no longer suffering: anxiety and hatred must have suddenly neutralised each other and erased all my painful feelings.

"How long do we have to visit the temples of Lambahadam? Excellent. Let's go."

Outside, awaiting the passengers, are three means of transportation: the carts drawn by zebu, those humped Indian oxen with long twisted horns which are bent over their backs and are painted with red and blue stripes; the rickshaws, those runabouts made of bamboo and pulled by the naked locals; the elephants, with their tall eight-seated howdahs—the hundred-year-old elephants, wrinkled as wineskins, also painted with lively colours, like old leather and covered with saddlecloths of silk or worn-out and faded velvet. No Europeans: only a crowd of indigenous people all around: nudity, the glimmer of white teeth, eyes already too big and made gloomier and deeper by bistre with an art unknown to our most refined ladies of the night; slim young girls wearing nothing but a little chain around their loins and a metal heart which

---

1 Camillo di Cavour (1810-1861) was the first Prime Minister of Italy. Casimiro Teja (1830-1897) was a popular caricaturist.

sways, in a very uncertain way, over the place that it should cover.

The town, made up of red or white one-storey houses, is clean and cheerful, buried in the trembling green of coconut palms and banana trees. The roofs are crowned with long strips of crows, green parrots, and endless tails of monkeys gathered in a morning consistory. Our ride puts us at the same level as the windows and, looking in, we can see a woman combing her hair, a mother reprimanding her child, a merchant counting his money, an image of Vishnu and a small statuette of twenty-armed Shiva or elephant-headed Ganesh. From the windows, men, women and children smile and bow with their hands at their foreheads in the Indian greeting.

"My luggage! My luggage!"

Memory, sleepy and almost erased by this new spectacle, is awoken with a very painful shock.

The howdah is full, with the two of us and six Indians, pilgrims travelling to the Temple of the Cloud.

And here is the temple.

One forgets everything. Above the undulating ocean of green coconut trees and against the turquoise sky, an immense golden structure rises up—terraces, spires, domes and flights of stairs overlap in a chaotic mass that overcomes and confounds every law of gravity, every architectural concept of proportion and regularity—a thing maybe three times taller than the Great Pyramid, a thing that could not be the work of man.

It is not the work of man. It is a boulder fallen from the sky onto the endless land of Hindustan, a geological oddity from primitive cataclysms. When Vishnu created the Earth, he found between his fingers a scrap left over from his work, so he rolled it up and threw it into the void and it fell on the plain of Lambahadam, where it formed a domineering four-hundred-metre block among the evil vegetation.

For thousands of years, men worked on it in the same way one might work on an elephant's tusk; the solid rock is completely perforated with tunnels, verandas, stairs and huge sanctuaries that open up within and, with sacred fires burning there continuously since time immemorial, are dedicated to the three thousand Gods of the Hindu mythology, which they are all covered, plated with real gold, since the faithful flock from all over India to offer with both hands jewels and coins.

One climbs the precipitous steps carved in zigzags along the vertical wall; below us is an endless green plain, confined by nothing but a circle of minor temples. Crows and sacred vultures circle around, with a deafening and hostile croaking. From within each sanctuary, come the sounds of wild preaching, of a hoarse tom-tom, a music that now becomes frightening like a hundred roars, now dying down so it is like the buzz of a dragonfly in agony.

"My luggage! My luggage!"

One is always climbing. We make our way along more verandas and corridors. Some Brahmins who are naked except for an area around their loins, but look more noble and impressive than gentlemen in evening dress, follow us with their absent eyes. They all have a trident of Vishnu on their foreheads, the same symbol that shines on the architrave of houses, on the palm tree trunks, on the heads of the elephants and zebu. Walking from the dazzling light into the deep sanctuaries, one finds oneself for a few moments in total darkness, before the votive lights become visible, the flaming fires in front of the deities, the glittering of the gold and of the gems on the many arms, on the tiaras, on the monstrous breasts, on the elephantine trunks. Pillars and monolithic arches carved like lace hang endlessly in the shadows, and from the dark vaults comes a continuous squeaking, the silent flapping of giant wings of black fabric: these are the vampire bats, which are as large as two outstretched human arms, and which hang by the thousands from the dark vaults during the day and at night raid the plantations for fruit.

We rest for around half an hour in the last sanctuary at the top of the temple, sitting in the semi-dark coolness, because outside the sun is already high and terrible.

My eyes have become accustomed to the darkness. I see deities around the crypts; each idol is enclosed in an iron cage, like tigers, and the burning brazier in front of them animates the frightful faces of the monsters with its trembling and bloody reflection.

"My luggage! My luggage!"

A man, a Hindu policeman, hearing my groans and seeing me holding my head in my hands, approaches me and kindly asks:

"Have the gentlemen received any wrong?"

"No, no wrongs." And my Parisian friend explains the reason for my distress. While they are talking, a Brahmin, a naked old man with a long white beard, gets up and addresses himself to the policeman who looks at us and smiles:

"Gentlemen, the High Priest of Aparapanda, the great priest of the Goddess of Things-Far-Away-from-the-Hand, suggests a votive offering for your luggage; the cost is little, one rupee, and the result is certain."

The policeman walks away smiling.

A votive offering to the Goddess of Things-Far-Away-from-the-Hand? But of course! Where is this lady? That one? I give a coin and bow to the horrible visage enclosed in one of the ancient cages. More priests gather round us in the shadows, attracted by the two impure ones paying respects to their deity. One by one they approach us, offering us their favours: A votive offering to the God Who Repels Cobra Venom? To the God Who Protects Against the Misadventures of Travel? To the Goddess of Fertility? To the God Who Repels the Evil Eye? To the Goddess Tharata-Ku-Wha: the Goddess-of-the-Enemy-No-More?

Alas! What have they done to the divine treasure of the Vedas! Into what kind of shameful idolatry has the sublime philosophical heritage of the Upanishads turned into, that essence of the Unspeakable, of the One, of the Absolute! An obscene market where all votive offerings find their own charlatan, similar to those European department stores where special shop assistants preside over the various goods!

"The Goddess-of-the-Enemy-No-More? What does that mean?"

"Death," the priest calmly replied, "or some other sort of destruction of whoever is troubling you."

The image of Tita Vinadio flashed through my mind, dreaming through his blondish side whiskers à la Camillo Cavour.

I was silent, but my Parisian friend was shouting with great enthusiasm: "*Mais très bien ça!* As for myself, I have at least twenty people in France who I would like to never see again!"

Laughing merrily, we approach the new altar. The high priest, who is even more decrepit and sinister than the previous one, cuts a rectangle from a large leaf of a palmyra palm and, offering it to me with an already dipped brush, signals me to write.

I write the name of Tita Vinadio and throw it onto the coals, which devour it with a crackle. Immediately, the bony hand offers me another leaf. Another victim? I don't have enemies. Who else should I get rid of? Ah, of course! Don Fulgenzi, the torment of our house. And so the name is written and devoured by the fire. The bony hand offers me still another sheet and I search through my dislikes . . . Ah, yes, that detestable fellow with the hooked nose—most definitely a jinx since every time I ran into him, usually on the tram, on the train or at the theatre, things would go wrong for me. So I write, "That detestable nameless fellow with the hooked nose."

"A fourth leaf! No, no! No more." I laugh, but the joke is starting to make me shiver with fear. Amidst the shadows, sinister idols and the screeching of the vampire bats.

But my Parisian friend is merciless. He writes and casts leaf after leaf into the fire, damning all his relations to the Goddess.

"Ma tante Véronique! Mon oncle Alexio! Mon cousin Frédéric! Mon cousin Ciprien! Mon ami Chautel!"

I grab him and take him outside into the sunlight; we go down the stairs laughing:

"*Combien en avez vous foutu?*"[1]

"Three."

"*Seulement?* Between family members and diplomatic colleagues, I rid myself of fourteen people!"

By evening, the train is already quite far from Lambahadam. My friend is hunched over the end of a table in the dining car, writing on the back of a menu a list of names and numbers. He grins.

"Pardon me, I'm done. I've made a list of the eliminated. Not counting the moral and material advantages due to the disappearance of five colleagues, upon my return to France I should find an inheritance of four million seven hundred thousand francs, if the Goddess Tharata-Ku-Wha grants me my wishes."

That night, no longer distracted by the landscape and the joking, I felt the anguish for my lost treasure again. Insomnia and desperation tormented me to the hectic rhythm of the train until dawn. I had been asleep for around an hour when I was woken up by the cheerful screams of my travelling companion. We had arrived at Kathalla.

"*Mon ami!* Quickly! Get off!"

I leapt off. Ten steps away from me, under a flowery veranda, I saw my nine boxes, piled up in a nice pyramid, sparking under the tropical sun with the beautiful colours of Italy.

---

1 "How many did you damn?"

At first, I touched them—thinking that I was dreaming, touched them for an extended period—and then I hugged the stunned station master, hugged an old Hindu lady who ran away in astonishment, holding her amulets, hugged my friend who was even more frantic than I, and, holding hands, we started turning around, our feet gradually joining together, our bodies becoming a dizzy spinning wheel.

"*Viva la Francia!*"

"*Vive l'Italie!*"

The station master separated us, tried to calm us down by taking us by the shoulders and forcing us to get back on the train, gently but with determination. I got on the train only after having received the double reassurance of vigilance and of an advanced telegraphic notice along the whole line to Bombay.

It was a delicious twenty-day journey with that ever-gay Parisian.

But in Bombay—we had to separate that day to embark to our different homelands—I saw him turn suddenly pale, a letter trembling in his convulsed fingers.

"*Ah! Les malheureux!*"

"So?"

"*Mes cousins . . .*"

"So?"

"They fell from the Guaslin monoplane . . . my uncle . . . has gone mad . . . it's hopeless!"

I was speechless. I heard the three names again, and again I saw the dark cave with the vampire bats and the Brahmin with the white-haired chest, the Goddess sneering behind the bars illuminated by the light of the bloody brazier.

I comforted my friend and accompanied him on board the ship which weighed anchor in the afternoon. Soon afterwards I embarked for Italy with all my luggage. I was happy.

Ten days later, however, in Aden, a letter from my mother was delivered to me on board which gave me an icy chill.

". . . I should be writing on black-bordered paper, but it would be hypocrisy, as you understand. Don Fulgenzi passed away three days ago . . ."

I was trembling. No! No! That Goddess! That temple! That spell! Two imprudent young men plunge from a thousand metres. The father goes crazy, a wicked old man has ceased making others suffer: isn't all this simply natural? Are you trembling? Have you too become an idiot or a theosophist? The lunch bell rang.

The light, the flowers, the glasses, the beautiful white shoulders, the cheerfulness of the officers, all made me regain a sense of reality. I blushed and laughed at myself. I wanted to forget. Eight days later, reaching Genoa, I had forgotten all about it.

Months went by.

Last autumn, in Venice, I was sitting on the divan in the middle of the Viennese Room, to rest a little and enjoy, at a distance and with eyes half-closed, a beautiful painting of a mermaid by Krawetz.[1]

---

1 The location of this scene is unclear, but it might well be the Doge's Palace. The artist is unknown, and likely an invention of the author.

But two visitors, standing very near the canvas, were taking away my pleasure; one, tall and dark, supported the other, who was small and bent: a little old man with blondish hair. The dark haired one turned and I recognised him. I walked towards him with affectionate warmth; it was Claudio Girelli, the painter. I looked at the old man: he wasn't old, he was ill.

"You are acquainted with our good Tita Vinaldo, aren't you?"

The sick man gave me his left hand through the right arm of the other: "My wwright . . . my wwr . . . right I can only give you like this . . ."

And, laughing and crying, he used his left hand to take his right hand out of his pocket. He held it out to me, inert, hanging down like something that was not his. He laughed and he cried. But only half his facial muscles obeyed his laugh and cry; the other half either remained immobile or twisted themselves into an asymmetrical ictus that reminded me of an ancient mask.

"This dear Gil . . . Gilelli," he continued with a teary smile, "takes me to the exhibitions, takes me to the elecl . . . elecl . . ."

". . . electrotherapeutic clinic of Professor Gaudenzi," the other concluded. "And who, in just a few days, will heal our good old Vinadio. It's getting late, we need to go."

Compassionately, Girelli raised Vinadio's hanging limb, returned the right hand to its pocket, placed an arm through his and held him up by the armpit. But before leaving, he looked at me, who had fallen back on the divan speechless.

"Don't tire yourself out in these silly rooms . . . you must still be worn-out from your trip. Your complexion doesn't look that well, either."

Am I going mad?

No, not yet. I will probably go mad the day that I find out about the certain death of my third victim. *The detestable fellow with the hooked nose.* I haven't seen him again. Lately, though, something terrible has been happening. I recognised on the tram and in the theatre a gentleman he used to often keep company with. It's difficult to resist the temptation of introducing myself to him and asking him politely what has happened to so-and-so, his friend . . .

And if the gentleman were to reply, "Oh, you didn't hear about it? Don't you know that he passed away a year ago?" I would jump off the tram, I would escape from the theatre, would burst into the police station to shelter my remorse, that of a triple-murderer, beneath the punishment of human justice.

But I'm certain that the good judge, after listening to my frantic confession and having taken into consideration that human law does not contemplate murder by vows to the Goddess Tharata-Ku-Wha, would comfort me with paternal words, and then, giving a nod to two loving guards, he would choose to send me not to prison but to the insane asylum . . .

The Real Face

"AND Nino Prandi?"

"Mad."

"No!"

"Raving mad. For nearly two years now he has been at the Villa Claudia, on the Colle D'Antale. It's over for him. . . . Of course, if you recall, he has always been rather odd."

"And his mother?"

"She died, a little before the catastrophe;—better for that fine old woman . . ."

"Nino mad! . . ."

"Exactly. Not even thirty years old, and already done with, having almost reached glory, wealth . . ."

"And have you seen him since?"

"No. Once, a long time ago, I went for an excursion in the country, to Vareglio di Sori. . . . With many women, many young ladies. Possibly too many. We were not allowed to see him. And I never went back. . . . In any case,"—and my friend lit a cigarette, sheltering the match inside the hollow of his hat—"in any case, the mad are like the dead, like the departed: they are no more; it's cruel, but one must forget about them; life is pressing . . ."

After the theatre, my friend and I, a journalist from Genoa, were walking down the windy Via Caffaro and he was telling me about everything that had changed in Italy during the two years of my absence. I had disembarked in Genoa a few days previous, returning from Libya, without glory and without wounds, with pronounced anaemia and pronounced sadness; but none of the sad news found in my homeland had struck me as much as this catastrophe.

The mad are like the dead: one must forget about them; life is pressing.

Ah! No! I wanted to see him again, be recognised, make him talk.

And the next day, alone and on foot, I took the same road to Vareglio d'Altano. I followed the path along the sea, closed in between the high walls of the patrician villas, walking with my head bent, distracted, absent, mechanically guided by the narrow red brick strip which marks the middle of all the lanes of seventeenth-century Genoa; the silence was being pointed out, rather than broken, by the echo of my rhythmic steps, by the distant roar of the dynamite intended since years previous to demolish the beautiful cliffs, to prepare new space for the town closed in between the mountain and the sea. And I remembered having passed along those same small lanes with Nino Prandi, years before, and recalled the artist's complaints about that tranquil dying suburb.

At intervals, the raw walls, defended on top by fragments of glass, sparkling under the lively March sun, would open up into gardens with palms and eucalyptuses, delimited by two zones of different cobalt—the sky and the sea. Poor Nino! What a strange and candid painter, what a pleasant friend!

He lived with his mother on Via Embriaci, below Ripa, in one of those immense human beehives, brightly-coloured, facing the port. He lived, despite his growing prosperity, in a neat and minute lodging, on the fifth or sixth floor, and from there one flight up to his studio—the terrace of the building, which had been converted into a huge conservatory from which it was possible to look over the Alps and the Apennines, the sky, the whole port, the entire sea. Almost no furniture, no decor; the flowers of the season renewed each day with fabulous abundance, some canvasses, the latest portrait on an easel, and between the verdure, well hidden, were the cages large and small, the boxes, the aquariums of his dear beasts: his mania, his menagerie. I do not know from what strange atavistic recurrence sprang this refined artist of a Genovese family of merchants: his father, who had been dead for years, if I remember correctly, had been a ship-owner from Camogli; his mother, together with certain relations, at that time ran a prosperous imports shop. According to the common ambition of merchants, they had wanted little Nino to become a graduate; but he, after his first years at University, left for the Academy, then almost immediately left the Academy for art, an art totally his own; a few paintings at the expositions of Venice, Paris and Munich confirmed him to be a great, a colossal artist, and at twenty-eight years of age he had the unique good fortune to see himself recognised by the most severe artistic circles and to see his work requested in the most aristocratic and wealthy social surroundings:

it was glory and riches: gold and laurels. But neither the one nor the other had changed that extraordinary, that simple and good-hearted young man in any way.

He was an exquisite connoisseur not only of paintings, but also of poetry, music and the natural sciences; he had that kind of Leonardesque quality which is indispensable—he would say—to all painters. He lingered meticulously over the smallest details of his paintings and meditated for a long while over the shading of a drop of water, over the elytra of an insect, over the geometrical exactness of a refracting ray. And he was not a poseur; elegant thought, refined observation were innate in him. With his family he spoke in the dialect of Genoa of the rarest things, and there was nothing I liked more than this contrast: noble thoughts, à la Ruskin, Maeterlinck and Oscar Wilde, expressed in the dialect of Balilla . . .

But animals were his great passion. He had converted his studio into a zoo well hidden among the flowers.

Visitors—ladies especially—passed hours in gay curiosity. He had a fox, a lynx, a squirrel, an ermine, a caiman, a giant squid, all the most distinctive birds, the most stylised—from the flamingo to the royal owl.

The painter guarded, personally looked after, with jealousy, his vast menagerie. And, his passion being notorious and his knowledge infinite, he often received specimens; and in the bright studio, the various sized cages and aquariums multiplied. Sometimes he appeared in front of us completely radiant.

"Have you sold the painting at the Salon? Will you do the portrait of the Queen of Holland?"

"Come now! I have received a young kangaroo from the Consul of Melbourne . . ." And he dragged us to see the new guest and for days, for weeks, would not talk of anything else, would not see anything else, neglecting his painting, disregarding his friends.

He passed hours and hours in front of his prisoners:

"It's very strange," he said, after long observation, "but each animal reminds one terribly of certain men."

On the street, he considered one by one the passers-by: ". . . and each man reminds one terribly of certain animals."

He did not smile. And he managed to carry this passion even into his paintings, even into his portraits. Next to a beautiful, elegant woman, between the silky spirals of her train, on the back of a chair, in a dark angle in the background, he accurately painted, although almost invisible, the animal that recalled the face of the protagonist.

He thus had a series of ladies and gentlemen *from the squirrel, from the lizard, from the seahorse*, etc.

On the face of the person being portrayed he laid a very light mask of animal-like sympathy with a symbolic little animal hidden in a corner of the painting, an expression just slightly perceivable to the initiates, his friends and accomplices, but of a really great finesse and irony. Sometimes the bestial caricature was very obvious indeed.

"Nino! You are exaggerating! They will sue you! It is impossible not to see that this gentleman is a toad, that this lady is a duck . . ."

But the gentlemen and the ladies did not see; and the fame and fortune of Nino Prandi grew.

When asked who it was that he was portraying, he answered seriously, which was for us quite amusing:

"The *Pangolin* will be finished next month;—it has turned out rather good;" (the pangolin was a *Miss*, incredibly long, sharp, elusive); "on Tuesday I will have the first sitting with the *Condor*: I will make something atrocious;" (the Condor was a Genoese financier: skinny, bald, fierce, with a long neck and goitre emerging simultaneously from the rich fur of his overcoat). "I had to refuse Countess Gribaudi: it's useless, I don't feel the *Platypus* . . ."

We laughed, but he did not. He did not even smile.

When he came to say farewell to me, to embrace me on the *Sardegna* before my departure for Libya, he begged me to bring him back a couple of chameleons.

Well then, in a few minutes I will see him again!

I went around the enormous Villa Riborsi, onto the Colle D'Antale, and there above, halfway up the hill, appeared the Villa Claudia, the madhouse, ironically gay and pretty, completely pink against the intense green of the pines.

Now that the destination was near I slackened my pace, I hesitated, panted—and not simply because of the ascent—the emotion made my heart beat fast, so very fast. I was soon to see him again, and to see an insane friend again is something terrible, as frightening as lifting up the slab of marble which closes off the corpse of someone who was once very dear . . .

And here I am in front of the door: I ring the bell with a trembling hand.

Hic quies hic sanitas is written above the architrave of the entrance. Nobody comes. I ring again; another electrical sound replies, more distant, and then a step, a jangling of keys, a great noise of bolts and the heavy door slowly opens, a door-keeper examines me with circumspection.

"Signor Nino Prandi? Is it possible to see him?"

"Come in; I'll call the director."

A long period in the banal waiting-room. I go out into the spacious garden, with laurels, pines and magnolias; the sad seclusion is very well hidden. The bars of the windows do not have the typical shape of a prison's, but are folded in leaves, flowers, liberty volutes; a plaster Diana bends her bow toward an invisible prey; through the open space between the verdure appears the blue trembling of the sea.

In the waiting-room I am met by the director, a squat figure, with a sharp face, terribly squinting eyes and a glabrous mouth, cloven all the way up to his extremely mobile ears.

"You are here to see Prandi? Who are you? A relative?"

"More than a relative. . . . It is not just curiosity, believe me. My visit might do him good."

"But he doesn't recognise—he doesn't recognise anybody!"

"He will recognise me. He cannot not recognise me!"

The director smiles, as if this was an absurdity.

I insist; he resigns himself to my demand, presses an electrical button, and an attendant appears; another strange figure—long, wiry, with an interminable neck surmounted by a microcephalic head on which only an enormous nose is encamped, curved, carnivalesque.

I would smile at these two diverse 'grotesques', but feel an anxiety, an invincible panic; I tremble slightly and now wish the director would deny the consent he has already given; instead he stands up, invites me with a gesture, and I must follow the two through rooms, corridors and galleries furnished with mysterious and disquieting electrotherapeutic devices.

"Is he raving?"

"No, not at all. He has a tranquil insanity, but complete and without a moment of clarity. Are you seeing him again for the first time?"

"Yes, since the catastrophe."

"Well then, we will find out what kind of beast *you* are . . ."

I started and looked at the director.

"What did you say? Explain to me . . ."

"It's not necessary, you will soon understand."

The two look at each other, laughing; the attendant cautiously opens the door of a room—candid, clean and sparsely furnished.

Nino Prandi sits at a writing-desk, in front of the window, with his back toward us as we enter.

I recognise him.

"Prandi! Oh! Prandi!"

He does not turn around. Not daring to advance, I stand on the threshold with the director. The attendant approaches Nino, takes him by the arm and, with gentle violence, forces him to advance, to turn toward us. And when he turns, I no longer recognise him.

Ah, that face is no longer his! It is true, just as one does not look upon corpses, so one should not look on the mad! That inanimate face becomes more and more spastic, and those eyes light up with a flash that might be the astonishment, the increasing joy of seeing me again! He recognises me!

"Do you recognise me? Prandi, it's me, I'm back! Safe and sound!"

He approaches, slowly—and I would flee, if I did not see that his arm is properly grasped by the attendant and if I did not have the director next to me. He approaches with his hand outstretched, as if for a light caress. Oh! how I shiver when his fingers graze my cheek, my hair . . .

"Prandi, do you recognise me?"

He speaks. But with such a voice! It is a voice that comes through a closed door, through a passage, defeated by echoes; he smiles with satisfaction.

"Are you happy to see me again, Prandi?"

With a blissful smile, he speaks.

"Ah, what a rarity! But this is a rarity. . . . It was believed to be lost forever . . . a telegraph must be sent to London . . ."

"But do you know who I am, Prandi? Answer."

The director intervenes.

"Answer my good fellow: who is this gentleman?"

The lunatic looks around dreamily, then gestures somewhat disapprovingly against the ignorance of the two.

"It is the *Alca inpennis*, a rarity . . ."

The two laugh, but I step back behind the threshold, annihilated.

The madman, seeing me escaping, attempts to follow, but is detained by the two hands of the brutal attendant. The door is being closed, and I can still hear that choked voice protesting: "The *Alca inpennis . . .* a rarity . . ."

I return to the study with the director, in silence, followed soon afterwards by the attendant.

"Has he calmed down?"

"No, Signor Director, he's in a frenzy. He'll be like this for at least an hour, so I have locked him up."

The director turns toward me, annoyed and satisfied at the same time.

"You see! Everything is in vain. Undoubtedly this form is incurable."

"But the causes? Atavistic?"

"I don't believe so. It's probably some sort of youthful breakdown aggravated by excessive intellectual work."

"But his frenzy of a moment ago?"

"Have you not understood? He also took you for a beast. Among his other manias he has one which I would call, *Zoomorphic*: every person appears to him with an animal-like face. He is not the first of this kind. The form is rare, but it is classified and studied: Professor Majer deals with it in his colossal work, and it is also dealt with by Professor . . ."

While the director was talking, I did not listen to his words, but observed his figure against the black background of the study, illuminated by a zone of oblique sunlight. Those circular, squinting and independent eyes, that depressed face, mouth cloven all the way up to his small pointed and extremely mobile ears, that double chin which trembled during his learned disquisition, what kind of beast could they ever evoke?

Truly none . . . well, no actually; maybe some sort of Antediluvian monster.

"But you, and others whom he is familiar with, how do they appear in his eyes?"

The Professor laughed loudly, shaking.

"Beasts; we are also beasts. Myself, for example . . . ? Well, I am not as formidable in natural science as your poor friend. Ah yes, I am an . . ."

"Maybe an *iguanodon*?"

"Ah yes, an *iguanodon*. . . . How did you know?"

The professor looked at me, perplexed. I was left speechless by my enormous and irreparable blunder, and also left speechless by the correlation of my own thoughts with those of the madman. I sprang out of my chair; my legs, trembling continuously, shamefully, hardly supported me.

The director smiled again, motioning toward the attendant. "This one, for example, is less rare: he is a *flamingo*." I rapidly looked over that profile, entirely nose, and shivered violently: it was true.

I went out, escaped from the lunatic asylum.

In the evening, in the silence, in the darkness of my bedroom, I could not fall asleep. Certainly I had a fever; my memory was tormenting itself to recall the name that my friend had given me. All of a sudden, the syllables flashed through my mind unexpectedly: *Alca inpennis*.

I stood up, switched on the light, opened the encyclopaedia, and found it almost immediately:

". . . *Alca inpennis* or *Patagonian Penguin*. Type of web-footed bird, today extinct. In the past, it inhabited Patagonia and Tierra del Fuego; its inability to fly and to walk, condemned it to a complete destruction; one specimen only, in poor condition, is being preserved in the London museum . . ."

The text was supplemented by a beautiful engraving: the border of an ice-bank, with the upright form of that strange bird which looked as if it were dressed in a man's dinner jacket. . . . But that high forehead, surmounted by a wavy tuft, that long and straight beak, that outstretched neck, were they not my exact caricature, that which had appeared in a humorous newspaper a few days ago?

Resolutely I carried the heavy volume over to the big triple-pane mirror and contemplated alternately my profile and the profile of the strange bird.

It was me!

I closed the mirror, laid down the volume and took refuge in bed, feverish, after having swallowed a double dose of sleeping potion. And sleep came quite soon, but webbed with indescribable dreams, like an immense, animated engraving of Speaking Animals.

Pamela Films

MADEMOISELLE OTTEMPATI (for many years, in the town, certain malicious people had been replacing the O with an A)[1] had a delicate, Goldonian first name: it was Pamela.

Pamela! A dimpled face, a Watteau profile, two deep eyes, two red lips, a triangular smile . . .

Alas! Pamela was sixty years old and possessed none of these qualities. But it was not time that had made her ugly. Whoever remembered her from when she had been twenty, remembered her as horrible and masculine, angular and bony, slightly hunch-backed and slightly lame, with the grotesque profile of some exotic web-footed bird: an enormous nose complicated by strange protuberances, a mouth cloven to the ears, tiny green eyes shielded by two eyebrows that were joined together into one, bushy and prominent like a type of moustache . . .

Nature is, in many cases, perverse. There is nothing more pitiful than to see certain people condemned to live their entire lives in a deformed body, like prisoners who, in a horrible prison, are expiating the sins of another.

---

1 The Italian word "attempata," means "old" or "aged" and might be used for a person, or a cheese.

Yet, when she had been twenty years old, Pamela Ottempati had had a ray of sunshine in her life. She had been engaged to a notary's secretary. Cruel destiny stole her betrothed from her, almost on their wedding night, by means of a fulminating pneumonia. From that day on, the virgin widow no longer shaved her hairy chin or bothered, with sprinkles of powder, to remove the livid shine from her nose. Time and religious practice had offered her consolation for that torment. Later, however, Pamela had the second, and possibly most serious, sorrow in her life: a quarrel with her brother, a handsome fellow who was much younger than herself, whose temperament was the very opposite, a man born for gain, pleasure, and adventure. The quarrel had dealt the poor spinster a tremendous blow. She saw herself cheated of the greater part of her possessions and was left alone in the old provincial home, with her dog, her cat, her chickens, and her maid. The years had soured her character, had made her implacable towards everybody and everything, tender only when it came to religion and charity. For fifteen years she had not seen her brother, though, from time to time, she did receive indirect news. He had been abroad, in France, in England, had increased his fortune, then ruined himself, then become rich once again, as a theatre manager, and later as a filmmaker. A lucky and eventful life, dissolute and sinful, of which Pamela did not want to know the slightest details. For three years the old spinster had been living in the greatest anxiety. Her brother had returned to Italy, had settled down in Turin and set up a large film company. And in these three years the company had prospered incredibly, and was considered one of the most important.

And so Pamela had become resigned to seeing her honest surname in the newspapers beneath the most iniquitous titles. Some of the company's films came to the movie theatre in Vareglio, and so, when Pamela walked by the large posters depicting crimes and embraces, brutal men and scantily dressed women, she lowered her eyes and furrowed her enormous eyebrows, murmuring ferociously:

"Dishonour as well! Grief, humiliation and dishonour!"

And for three years she had given up her already infrequent walks through town. And had not ever seen her brother again, or forgiven him.

Even when he suddenly died, she did not forgive him.

The death of the great magnate caused a general sensation; it was written about in the newspapers and talked about at length in the film world. In the small provincial town, they spoke of nothing else:

"Forty-three years old!"

"Such a handsome man!"

"Almost a millionaire!"

"A voluptuary!"

"Strong and healthy!"

"But he had a temper!"

"Apoplexy!"

"Fulminating!"

In fact, death had grabbed hold of him while he had been on a train, between Genoa and Nice, taking a few days off for relaxation—a romantic holiday with the divinely beautiful movie star Diana Carmeli, who a starving poet being fed by the company had once called "The Duse of silence."[1]

Miss Pamela did not want to hear about it, did not want to know about it. She was horrified. She did not cry for her brother, but did not know how to console herself for that reckless death which had brought to an end a most reckless life, shivering in the certainty that his soul was lost.

"Pray, pray for his peace. It will be a great comfort to you."

"Pray for his peace? He died in damnation!"

"No one has the right to say this, signorina," the priest, who was less severe and implacable than his follower, observed. "No one can know what happens to a soul at the time of its last farewell."

Miss Ottempati would not be comforted. She adjusted a cheap bluish bandeaux over her moustache-like eyebrows, petted her decrepit dog Bob and, sighing disconsolately, repeated to herself:

"Damned! Damned for eternity!"

A week after the death, Pamela received a letter from solicitor Quinteri.

---

1 A reference to the actress Eleonora Duse. She had love affairs with both Arrigo Boito (Camillo Boito's younger brother) and Gabriele d'Annunzio, the latter writing four plays for her to appear in.

He was an old friend of the family, loyal and extremely trustworthy, who had already assisted her, many years previously, during the vicissitudes with her brother, without having a great deal of success.

After a few words of condolence, the lawyer allowed himself—in consideration of old trust and friendship—to ask her if she was thinking of doing anything regarding the legal formalities, and, once again, put at her disposal, should they be needed, all his services and advice in the difficult circumstances.

"Difficult circumstances?"

"The inheritance, signorina," the old servant commented. "You are the only heir. You see, I was right . . ."

The inheritance of that scoundrel. . . . Pamela did not sleep all night and at dawn awoke more frightened than ever.

"I'm going. It is necessary that I go to the lawyer and talk with him right away. Give me my things."

In front of a large and murky Empire mirror, Pamela put on her town clothes: a blouse with lace and beads, an immense gown (despite the passing of time and changes in fashion, she had never given up her three starched petticoats and funnel-shaped corset). On her shoulders she fitted a carmen cape, model 1890; on her false and stringy hair she arranged a frail little hat on which three squalid peacock feathers lodged in a parrot's head trembled.

"You will be needing to think about clothes for mourning."

"I will think about that when I get to the city. I imagine I will need to stay for a few days. Who knows what news is waiting for me there!"

"News that will console you! How I wish I was in your place, signorina!"

"But who can say what troubles lie ahead."

"With Quinteri, you can be sure everything will be fine."

Pamela Ottempati put a collar and festive-looking leash on Bob and left, sighing:

"May God be good to me!"

Pamela was at a loss to explain the signs of attention she received on the streets of the city.

"So much curiosity for one person from out of town! They are more gossipy in the city than the country," she murmured ferociously to herself, looking furtively at the street urchins, the young men, the ladies who stopped and turned as she walked by.

"After all, I'm not a monster and am not going about dressed like some of these other shameless creatures . . ."

To escape that inexplicable trail of admiration, she took a cab. While waiting in solicitor Quinteri's office, she luxuriously breathed in the notary atmosphere: the smell of soured ink, the putrid stench of stamped paper, which took her back to when she had been twenty, to her hopes, and her deceased love.

Alas! In front of her stood the potbellied lawyer, talking to her in a solemn tone, his eyes on the ceiling, the five fingers of one hand pressed against the five fingers of the other:

". . . You mustn't worry. You have four months for the inheritance notification, for the judiciary certificates necessary to bring you into the peaceful possession of the substance that your poor brother left behind when he passed away. Fate is giving you back, with interest, what was previously taken from you."

"Fine, but where is all this money?"

"As far as ready money goes, there is not much—maybe forty thousand. Most of the assets—around eight hundred thousand liras—are invested in the studio."

"Then liquidate it right away."

"Liquidate? But it would be madness! We couldn't get a fifth of its value."

"Find a buyer. I don't want to be the owner of such an unseemly place."

"An unseemly place? But you are mistaken, my dear lady. Ottempati Films has the reputation of being in the moral and artistic vanguard of the industry. Would you care to think about it a while? And first maybe bestow a visit on the place?"

"Will you accompany me?"

"I will accompany you. You are staying at the Hotel Concordia, right by the studio. We'll meet tomorrow, at nine-thirty, in front of it. Does this suit you?"

At nine o' clock the next morning Miss Ottempati, with large strides, was already pacing the small piazza in front of the open gates. In one hand she twirled a massive umbrella, in the other she held Bob's leash.

She hazarded a look inside the immense courtyard. A number of things attracted her attention: some monkeys in a cage, a large bed of roses in bloom, two children dressed as pages who were playing with a greyhound.

Timidly she ventured within, visited her imprisoned sisters, inhaled a rose without picking it, and petted a child who ran away laughing. When she turned around to go, the gate was obstructed by a number of cars from which a squad of Napoleonic soldiers were getting out. They seemed to turn towards her, to be greeting her from afar:

"Tulipier!"

"Hello Tulipier!"

"Bravo Tulipier!"

They laughed and screeched. Were they talking to her? Bewildered, she escaped through a tiny door, walked through a dark passage, and came out in a bright corridor, before trying to go through another gate, which was closed. She turned back, passed between two eighteenth-century backdrops, and was lost.

"Tulipier, listen! . . ."

The voices followed her, echoing. She escaped, almost at a run, along corridors, and came out in an immense glass structure that was divided into small backstage theatres, crowded and complicated like a labyrinth. A few Roman soldiers blocked her way. She ran. She found herself in a ball room, among women in low-necked dresses and gentlemen in *ispirato*. A cameraman yelled at her in anger:

"Tulipier! Get out of here! You are ruining my scene, you fool."

Pamela stepped back, veered to the right, into group of fakirs and Indian dancing girls. All ways of escapes were shut off, she saw herself lost, leaned against an altar of Vishnu and then turned to defend herself, with Bob, barking furiously, held tightly in the pit of her arm, and the massive umbrella twirling in her right hand.

Her bearded chin trembled. A quaking agitated her enormous eyebrows and the little hat with its three miserable feathers. Soldiers of Julius Caesar, soldiers of Napoleon, and Brahmins, circled around her, cheering:

"It's Tulipier! What an artist!"

"Such a great make-up job!"

"It doesn't seem like make-up at all!"

"He looks like an actual witch!"

"Bravo Tulipier! Hooray for Tulipier!"

A Brahman priest, more enthusiastic than the rest, grabbed her around the knees and lifted her up, above the excited crowd. Pamela let out a scream and fainted in the arms of solicitor Quinteri, who had just then arrived.

"You rascals! What are you doing? This is Miss Ottempati, the new owner."

Soon after, in the quiet of the managerial offices, comforted with cordials and words, Miss Ottempati recovered her senses. She refused to resume her visit to the studio and refused the car that was offered her. She wanted to leave the place where she had been insulted as soon as possible, the persuasive words of solicitor Quinteri being of no avail.

And the next day and the day after that and forevermore, Pamela was obstinate.

"Liquidate—sell the place for whatever you can."

A British-American firm realised that they could get a good deal. Within a week they had purchased the studio for three hundred thousand liras. Pamela received this treasure with a shiver of joy and fear. She was, however, able to cleanse herself of any scruples by donating twenty-five thousand liras towards the building of the Vareglio Hospital, and another twenty-five thousand to the Society for the Protection of Young Women.

And so once again was proven, in the fluctuation of human deeds (according to the teachings of the theosophists) the law of perfect equilibrium.

The Handsome Hound

"THAT WOMAN is looking at you!"

"She loves me!"

It was noon, the fashionable time of day on that tram line, when the well-to-do crowd was brought back to the most aristocratic suburb of the city. And the passenger car, in the frigid winter weather, smelled of fine furs, violets, and essences, like the automobile of some aristocrat.

"But she really is looking at you!"

"She is in love with me. Does it surprise you so much?"

The handsome Claudio Serra staggered along the passageway, barely missed putting his friend's eye out with his cigarette, and almost stabbed a respectable looking gentleman in the kidneys with his ice skates.

"Don't fall over with excitement."

"I won't. I'm used to it. This is the tenth time that I have run into her at this time of day, and she always looks at me in that manner. She must have come to Turin not long ago, and probably lives in one of the houses on the new Piazza d'Armi . . ."

Claudio smiled broadly, showing a mouthful of dazzling teeth.

"And now you are smiling simply in order to show off your beautiful teeth," his ugly and implacable friend observed. "You look like a toothpaste advertisement."

"Idiot!"

"And now you are turning in profile, in order to show off your perfect nose. You look like the figure of Italy by Leonardo Bistolfi on the nickels."[1]

"Idiot!"

Claudio was perfect in two things: beauty and ice-skating. In ice-skating he had won, in his time, the highest honours: first place in the international competition. And his beauty was the type that made everyone, both men and women, turn their heads, reminding one of a Roman centurion refined by modern elegance, stylised by a London tailor. Twenty-four years old, rich, a good lad, extremely foolish, extremely vain, extremely sensual: and women adored him.

"But see how she is looking at you! It's indecent."

Claudio turned, caught in the eyes of the stranger such evident abandonment that it made him blush, and averted his gaze, most disturbed.

"You are blushing like a schoolgirl!"

"It isn't true!"

But Claudio was now blushing even more.

The unknown woman was sitting at the far end of the carriage, neglected in a corner, taking refuge in an immense black fox fur coat, at the bottom of which emerged a short and insufficient dress, tiny feet in masculine shoes;

---

1 Leonardo Bistolfi (1859-1933) was a sculptor. In 1907 he designed a nickel, one side of which showed the figure of Italy in profile.

and up high, two fine strips of black hair and two black eyes protected by a small, unadorned velvet hat.

She was extremely elegant. But her eyes were not at peace. Irises of blurred onyx rotating in an almost cerulean enamel, from right to left, from bottom to top, before being imperiously veiled, with an obvious effort of the will, by lowered lashes, before suddenly turning, with an ingenuous simulation of sudden curiosity, to the snowy landscape—almost instantly returning to the young man, with a passion and tenderness that forgot everyone else and all else.

"A well-mannered lady?"

"I would say so."

"How old do you think she is?"

"Forty."

"No! Thirty-five, at the most."

"Well, if it makes you happy, we can say thirty-five— but she *is* forty."

"Certainly, since she isn't looking at you, you ugly lecher!"

However, his ugly friend was right. Despite her youthful grace, black hair, and beautiful eyes, the woman was no longer young. When the sun reverberated off the snow, colliding with her violently, her fatigued chin, tired profile, and slightly hollowed cheeks appeared—the first signs of old age.

"Even with all this, she is still very desirable."

"I don't deny it. Look, she's getting off . . ."

Having rung the bell, the unknown woman rose from her seat, uncertain, before talking to the porter and getting off from the front gangway.

"Did you see that? She didn't want to come this way to get off. She was afraid that she might faint if she passed near you."

Claudio Serra turned and saw the lady, already far away, in a big snowy clearing, standing motionless, still staring at him.

"You have to do something."

"You're right. I'll follow her."

Without saying goodbye to his friend, Claudio jumped off the tram, which continued on at a dizzying speed.

The lady was in the distance, now walking hurriedly. The young man followed her, almost at a run. They were in a new neighbourhood: brand-new villas and villas still under construction amidst an expanse of snow: an unfamiliar and difficult terrain.

In order to catch up to the woman, Claudio had to cut across a field diagonally, sinking up to his ankles in snow. Two times he fell to his knees in the slush. He rose to his feet and bumped his knee against his sharp, heavy skates.

"Damnation!"

He gently rubbed the painful area and continued on, running, limping a little. The seductress had disappeared.

She reappeared near the edge of a lawn. Claudio hurried on, gaining ground. The lady was fleeing from him, frightened, almost running. She came to the door of a house, a luxurious villa, and raised her hand to ring the bell, but then, seeming to measure the distance that separated her from her pursuer, refrained—turned and put her back against the door, like one determined to fight with some nocturnal aggressor.

Claudio Serra stood in front of her; his skates in one hand, his hat in the other—more handsome, more foolish than ever.

"Madam . . ."

"Sir . . ."

They were both out of breath, unable to find words.

"Sir, there seems to be a misunderstanding . . ."

She was from Tuscany. Her novel manner of speech baffled Claudio even more—he, an illiterate subalpine, did not fancy women who spoke well.

"A misunderstanding that must be cleared up at once . . ."

"But no, Madam, I'm flattered . . ."

"Flattered by what?"

With all his splendid teeth, Claudio smiled.

"You're right. I stared at you too much and too tenderly, is it not so?"

" . . ."

"And you could believe? At my age? Ah! But we are nowhere near each other on this! What a disappointment for you! What a disappointment for me also, because your voice . . . your eyes . . . and yet, up close, you hardly seem like him at all . . ."

The lady lifted up her golden purse from which hung charms and tiny tools, looking for a round, jewelled pendant, which she opened, and put under the eyes of the perplexed young man.

"Don't you see the similarity?"

"To whom?"

"To yourself."

Claudio had spent a third of his life in front of the mirror and, knowing himself well, had to agree.

"Truly. It could be my portrait."

"No, it's of my son."

Claudio, bewildered, looked at the woman who was looking at him with moist eyes. He muttered an inopportune compliment.

"Please, don't become poetic with me! I am forty-three years old and can openly confess that, since they killed him, I am no longer a woman—am no longer of this world!"

She opened up an internal window on the device with her fingernail.

"Here he is when he was a boy of four; and at twenty when he graduated in law; and here he is as a second lieutenant . . ."

This last photograph had the place, date and fatal cross: The Battle of two Palms. Libya. March 12, 1912.

The lady rang the bell; the door opened at once, automatically:

"I would invite you in, but I am not at my own home. I am, for a short while, a guest of my cousins."

Claudio bowed his head, the expression on his face so contrite that the woman had pity, and kept the door ajar, looking at him

"Poor child, forgive me . . ."

"Of course!"

The lady stood, considering him in his grotesque embarrassment. Smiling between her tears, she was already taken hold of, already distracted by her incurable Florentine wit.

"It's strange . . . up close you don't remind me of him anymore. Walk a bit further away . . ."

Claudio obeyed.

"One more step. . . . There, like this the illusion is perfect. It breaks my heart. Come nearer . . . just so. And you no longer look like him. . . . But don't be disconcerted! It's strange, at six steps away you make me cry, but at two steps . . ."

"At two steps?"

"At two steps you make me laugh."

And they both did.

She talked a little more, with the door nearly closed.

"Let me look at you like that when we meet, look at you from a distance—this is the only way you are dear to me."

Claudio attempted to reply with a dramatic recollection.

"A statue of flesh, so then . . ."

"Precisely," the bizarre Florentine corrected. "A living puppet!"

And the door closed.

La Bela Madamin

ON the hills of Maddalene, which look over Turin, in a farmhouse that was once an old villa, I hopelessly beg a woman who is deaf to my every flattery.

Deaf, also, because the day before yesterday she celebrated her seventy-ninth birthday.

She is beautiful.

Against a large window made up of small square panes, the silver of her wavy hair sparkles like the silver of the alpine peaks behind her, and her beautiful face looks young, as if modelled in a reddish clay on which the stick of a great sculptor has put a few sudden wrinkles; her eyes of pure turquoise have an extremely youthful gleam in them, ironic and vigilant.

Her daughter, granddaughter, and grandson, who are all busy in the large kitchen, are laughing at me as I hold the hands of *granda*[1] and sit on a low stool at her feet, repeating for the tenth time my supplicating offer:

"I will add another ten—no, fifteen liras."

The old woman has not understood. Her granddaughter comes up and in her ear pronounces: "He is adding

____

1 Turinese dialect: grandmother.

fifteen liras." The old woman hesitates. Then, getting up, she turns to the women with a smile and a sigh, pointing at the pendulum-clock and to me:

"Ah, what a *balengo!*"[1]

Hearing assent in her insult, I rejoice.

In a page from one of her grandson's books, the old lady wraps the tiny *Robert*,[2] a delight in bronze and enamel, with the pot-bellied grace of the eighteen-century, escaped somehow from the sacking of the antique dealers. My joy is such that I almost don't hear the old lady singing, undoubtedly in order to console herself for the departure of a thing dear and familiar, her voice so young and harmonious that it seems not to belong to her, that it seems to come from another room:

> *La bela madamin la völo maridè,*
> *che al Düca di Sassònia i so la völo dè.*

But what is it? *La Bela Madamin*, the song of Carolina of Savoy, is then still sung on our Turinese hills? I had once studied it when researching subalpine folklore, becoming familiar with it through Nigra's[3] versions, but was under the impression that it was some fossil of popular literature. Listening to it, I rejoice, surprised as a paleon-

---

1 Turinese dialect: fool.

2 A clock, probably referring to one associated with the one of the inventions of Robert Hooke.

3 Constantino Nigra (1828-1907) was a diplomatist and scholar who published a number of works on folklore and popular poetry, the most well-known of which was *Canti popolari del Piemonte* [Folk Songs of Piedmont].

tologist suddenly finding himself before some wonderful species, alive and well beneath the light of the sun, that he had believed to be extinct.

And here I am sitting on a low stool, transcribing the verses on the back of the package containing the clock:

> *La bela madamin la völo maridè,*
> *che al Düca di Sassònia i so la völo dè.*
>
> *—O s'a m'è bin pi car ün pover paisan*
> *che 'l Düca di Sassònia ch' a l'è tant luntan!*
>
> *—Un pover paisan l'è pa del vostr onur!*
> *'l Düca di Sassònia a l'è ün gran signur.*
>
> *'l re cön la Regina l'an piàla bin për man,*
> *a San Giuan l'an mnàla, en Piassa San Giuan.*
>
> *—Da già che a l'è cusì, da già ch'à l'è destin,*
> *faruma la girada anturn a tüt Türin.*
>
> *—Cara la mia cügnà, perchè che piuri tant?*
> *Mi sun venüa da'n Fransa ch'à l'è d'co bin luntan.*
>
> *—Vui si venüa da'n Fransa, vui si venüa a Türin*
> *in Casa di Savoia, ch'a l'è 'n t'in bel giardin.*
>
> *—Cara la mia cügnà andè pür volontè,*
> *che drinta a la Sassònia a fa tanto bel stè!*

—Cara la mia cügnà tuchè-me'n po' la man:
Tüt lon che v'racomandö s'à l'è la mia maman.

Tuchè-me'n po' la man, me cari sitadin,
Për vive che mi viva vëdrö mai pi Türin![1]

---

1 Turinese dialect. The song is translated as follows:

Her parents want to give, to marry the young
and beautiful lady, to the Duke of Saxony.

"Oh, how I would prefer a poor farmer
to the Duke of Saxony who lives far away!"

"A poor farmer isn't of your rank!
The Duke of Saxony is a great gentleman."

The King and Queen took her by the hands,
and brought her to the Church of San Giovanni, on the
    Piazza San Giovanni.

"Since it is so, since it is destiny
we will take a turn around all of Turin."

"Sister-in-law, my dear, why do you cry so much?
I came from France, which is far away."

"You came from France, you came to the House of the Savoy
in Turin, which is a beautiful garden."

"Sister-in-law, my dear, go happily there,
since in Saxony one can live so very well!"

"Sister-in-law, my dear, hold my hand for a while:
All I have to offer you is my mother.

"Hold my hand for a while my dear citizens,
For as long as I live, Turin I will see no more."

And do you know who the *Bela Madamin* was? The King's daughter.

"Which King?"

"The King of Savoy."

"And the sisters-in-law? And the Duke of Saxony?"

The old lady and the ladies don't know anything more. But is it necessary to know?

Nothing harms poetry so much as facts, just as nothing is more favourable to it as perfect ignorance.

I leave, descending towards Turin, which shows itself through a curtain of three colours: pink, violet, and green, offset by the sinuous silver of the river, and the delicate silver of the Alps. I am happy. I whistle and sing. Under my arm, I have the beautiful bronze object. The beautiful words are in my ears; and I think that both things date back to approximately the same epoch, are both equally old—but that which is made of words is livelier, fresher than the one made of metal . . .

La Bela Madamin! Princess Maria Carolina Antonietta of Savoy, daughter of Victor Amadeus III, married by the proxy of her brother Carlo Emanuele to Prince Antonio Clemente, Duke of Saxony. . . . I know everything about her and her short and innocent life: I know dates, names, episodes, and numbers. I must be careful not to recall them in this hour of poetry. And once again I will ask my imagination—since only imagination can do what is impossible for all else, even God—to bring back the past.

And so the Turin of the present day disappears.

I go down to the plain. Where am I? I no longer recognise the suburb on the other side of the Po, am unable to find the temple of the Gran Madre.[1] I'm lost in a wild and archaic forest—even the trees and clouds have a different style. Above, the clouds mingle together with the branches of oaks and elms, creating a corridor on the fatiguing, badly maintained road—and these, which too well imitate Gobelins and tapestries, are not trees of our time. . . .

I get my bearings. To my left, atop wild vegetation, I see the Monte dei Cappucini; to my right, the Basilica di Superga[2]. . . . Superga. Which means that we are at some point after the mid-1700's. Walking along the river, I feel that it is certainly the Po, but it is without banks, primitive, it too from another period. . . . And Turin? A frightening shiver courses through me, that of a dream, when one sees things that are familiar, but they are strangely deformed by nightmare.

And there is the city. Turin?

On the opposite bank of the river, stands a bulwark of blood-coloured bricks crowned with granite; it raises itself up, now in mass, now with its sharp edges, embrasures, casemates, and cannons, and beyond the bulwark, appear roofs, domes, bell-towers and towers. . . . But

---

1 The Church of the Great Mother of God. One of the most important churches in Turin. Its construction was completed in 1831.
2 A church situated on the highest hill overlooking Turin—the hill of Superga. Its construction was completed in 1731.

Turin? Yes. The dome of the Metropolitana, the bell-tower of San Lorenzo, the Santi Martiri. . . . But, what frightening melancholy! It seems like one of those dark and minuscule towns that saints hold out on the palm of their extended hands . . .

In this kingdom of being-no-more, I am frightened; the ghosts of things are more terrible than the ghosts of people.

But I see people, I see men—soldiers—an Aosta brigade squad. They seem as if alive—white gaiters, red waistcoats, blue jackets, three-pointed blue hats trimmed with gold and coquettishly marked by the presence of white cockades; and their white wigs make their eyebrows, eyes and moustaches appear especially black and imperious. I follow the men as far the bridge—a strange bridge, half of which is made of wood and the other half suspended on two old crumbling arches—frail, shaky, as picturesque as some Flemish motif. Farmers dressed like Gianduja cross over, as does an acrobat with a perambulator and a monkey, and a Berlin carriage in which ride two abbots wearing huge hats, in the style of Don Basilio.[1]

I see a door of magnificent baroque architecture—the Porta Padana, the door to the Po! I shall then get to the Piazza Vittorio. I go through, but the Piazza Vittorio is no longer there, has not yet come to be. The town begins where today the Via Po ends. And finally I see the Via Po!

It has the same arcades, buildings, and balconies of wrought iron as in the present day, but it is deformed by

____

1 The music teacher from Rossini's *The Barber of Seville.*

I don't know what—there is something missing that I can't explain—possibly it is the lack of paving stones and pavement, of rails, and the Dora,[1] the stream that runs through its centre—and the scarcity, the poverty of the shops, that lend the road this sinister look of famine and pestilence.

And yet the street is brightened by two great triumphal arches made of wood and canvas, with allegorical baroque figures on them, and in its centre, the coat of arms of the House of Savoy with an anagram written in cursive beneath it. The crowd is large and gay—Gianduja and Giromette;[2] farmers flocking into the city, on this day, without a care in the world—bourgeoisie, gentlemen, soldiers on foot and on horseback, with flashing eyes and teeth, contracted lips and eyebrows, rough plebeian wigs, black or chestnut, the frizzy, silver-coloured wigs of nobles, a flexing of calves, both muscular and thin, in stockings of cotton and silk, of Giandujas or marquises, Berlins and sedan-chairs out of which shine the red of the make-up, the artificial black of beauty-spots, a mouth that smiles, a hand that whisks a fan or pets a little Chinese dog.

I question a soldier: he doesn't reply; a farmer: he doesn't even turn his head; an abbot: he doesn't look at me, doesn't bat an eye. And then I become aware of something unheard-of and terrible: they are shadows (or am I a shadow?) separated from me by the mystery of not-being-anymore, of not-yet-being.

---

1 The Dora Riparia.
2 Traditional Turinese carnival figures.

I see, but am not seen, hear but am not heard. . . .
Around me, they are speaking either French or old
Piedmontese, which has a very tight, Frenchified "r", or
the heavy Italian of printed books; so, in front of me, a
certain Count Dellala di Beinasco and a certain gentleman by the name of Mattè, an engineer, are deploring,
". . . the fatal inopportune rain that last night damaged the
machine of the joyous fireworks, the fireworks of cascades
and shapes most dreamy and delightful, so the embellished
young lady chose to draw an inauspicious omen . . ."

A little further on, at the corner of the Via San
Francesco da Paola, a public clerk reads a bill on a wall
aloud to a group of reverent illiterates: ". . . Before its
departure, the bridal procession will pass through the
city of Turin—coming out of the Palace of the Piazza San
Giovanni, it will go through the Via Dora Grossa, the
Piazza Castello, the Via Nuova, the Porta Nuova, and the
Porta di Po, the King and Queen granting the longing pub-
lic the favour of, once more, seeing the Beloved Imperial
Daughter. —September 29th, in the year 1781."

I also read the list of the, "sumptuous wedding gaie-
ties of the lofty marriage, etc., of Madama Carolina with
the Duke of Saxony represented by proxy by the bride's
brother. Yesterday, at the Castle of Moncalieri, the wedding took place. Today, the new Duchess of Saxony will
leave for Dresden, after taking a final tour of farewell
around Turin."

> *. . . Da già ch'à l'è cusì, da già ch'à l'è destin*
> *faruma la girada anturn a tüt Turin . . .*

La bela Carulina . . . la bela madamin. . . . Around me people speak in low voices about some sort of scandal that occurred yesterday during the solemn hour of the "yes" by the sixteen-year-old bride.

"Oh, Marquis, yesterday we had hoped to see you at Moncalieri."

"I did not receive an invitation."

"But this is impossible!"

"But it is so, Monsignor. I have already remonstrated the Master of Ceremonies. . . . Were there many people?"

"Not many. Maybe a hundred guests. The King, the Queen, Princess Carlotta of Carignano, Cardinal Marcolini, the Prince of Salm Salm, the Bishops, the Knights of the Order, the Prince of Masserano, the Ministers of State, the Captain of the Body Guards, the Master of Ceremonies Governor of the Prince, the Heralds, and the Persuivants of Arms of the Ambassadors."

"And the bride and groom?"

"They were not happy. First, the idea of separation evermore. And then, a child not yet sixteen years old married through her brother to a prince that she has never even seen . . ."

"Was she restless?"

"No, no. She demonstrated, so to speak, resignation. When the moment of the 'yes' came, she understood that her exile had been enacted, a lifetime exile, in that Saxony that must appear to her like the extreme Thule."[1]

---

1 Thule is the ancient name given to a mysterious land in Northern Europe, originally described by the Greek navigator Pytheas. The term "extreme Thule" or "ultima Thule" is used to denote a place extremely far away.

"But she was not restless?"

"Not at all; it took but a moment. The Grand Elemosiniere of the King came out from the sacristy in a pontifical manner and knelt at the altar and bowed to the King and the Queen and then asked the bride and groom the usual questions. The Prince of Piedmont replied at once; but the Princess, becoming pale, rose to her feet, staggered, and turned to her parents who were kneeling behind her—the look in the eyes of His Majesty subjugated her, bent her, made her kneel and burst out not with one but with three 'yeses' which made the whole court laugh. . . . Between us, Monsignor, today I would not want to be in the shoes of Count Lamarmora."

"Why?"

"Because, under the eyes of the King, he has assumed all responsibility for this farewell tour done to please the Queen and Princess. As you know, until last Saturday it was agreed that soon after the wedding, the retinue, accompanied by the Ambassador of the Elected Court of Dresden, would continue on directly to Moncalieri without stopping in Turin and go to Augusta, where the Commissars of the King of Savoy were to give the bride to the Commissars of the Duke of Saxony. It would have been the best choice. However, the Princess, poor child, looked for any excuse to put off her departure for an hour. She implored—she longed to stay in Turin for one more day and the Queen had the idea of a farewell promenade around the city accompanied by a showing of the Holy Shroud[1] in the Gallery of the Piazza Castello. The King

---

1 The Shroud of Turin.

was at first resistant, but then conceded, making Count Lamarmora, intercessor, responsible for the event, in order to avoid any possible problem. You well know how foreign scandals are to His Majesty. I do not wish to be a poor prophet, but would not be surprised if Princess Carolina goes into convulsions right in the middle of the Piazza Castello or the Via Dora Grossa. Yesterday, during the gala ball, she had the eyes of someone in a trance . . ."

"*Povra masnà!*"[1]

We are in the Piazza del Castello, an eighteenth-century piazza quite similar to that of today, yet also very different. It is lit by an incorrect sun—a sun which lights up old prints and things told in stories. . . . Two baroque arcades stretch out along the sides of the Palazzo Madama, dividing it in two; the lack of pavement and rails, of electric globes and metallic entanglements, signs and advertisements on the walls, gives it a stark, dead appearance. . . . How we moderns get life from all those things!

A huge crowd is pouring in through the Portici della Fiera—a strange crowd, set down and copied in copper engravings and Savona kitchenware (it is not art which imitates life, but life which imitates art;[2] nothing exists until is brought to light by artists); and over there is a carriage with four headstrong horses who are being reigned

---

1 "Poor girl!"
2 Reminiscent of Oscar Wilde's aphorism: "Life imitates Art far more than Art imitates Life."

in by a postilion—over there is the ducal sedan-chair, a servant leading a dog on the leash, two abbots who meet and shake hands, a mother reprimanding her child, some comedians in their booths, a charlatan who sells the elixir of long life, a sibyl who predicts the future. And the crowd is disposed according to the agreed upon taste that the Flemish painters brought to Piedmont, and the song of the day surges through it, in a vague, insistent rhythm.

Beyond the Palazzo Madama, hiding from view the other half of the Piazza, are the white clouds of acute-smelling incense, and a different murmuring rises up, a liturgical and solemn melody. I push myself through to the Arcades and stand still, captivated by the most solemn picture that intact faith has ever offered to mortal eyes.

The whole Piazza fluctuates with an indescribable multitude and has been converted into a temple which has the sky for its cupola. At the lower end, the loggia which separates the Piazza Castello from the Palazzo Reale rises up, and each arcade is taken up by an officiating bishop.

From the central arcade, protected by a vermilion canopy, the Holy Shroud hangs taut, the relic exposed to the crowd for a few hours—a treasure unique on this earth, the shroud in which Joseph of Arimathea wrapped the Redeemer's body after it had been taken down from the Cross.

And a thousand lips sing the *Te Deum*, and a thousand eyes stare at the double image of the Divine Body. Since morning, they have been celebrating in the open air and sunlight; the whole population praying out loud for the young lady from Savoy who in a few hours will be departing for a distant land.

Between the baroque columns of the high loggia, the bishop's mitre sparkles, damasks and silks, purples and sables stand out—the Clergy of the City, the Knights of SS. Maurice and Lazarus, the Knights of the SS. Annunziata, the Canons, Deacons, Mace-Bearers, Train-Bearers, Mayors, Decurions . . .

But *La Bela Madamin* of the song?

The royal canopy is empty. The court has just retired for the last palace ceremonies and the audiences of leave.

La Bela Madamin! . . . I want to see her . . .

I enter the Palace. Alas, even for a pure invisible and imponderable spirit it is not easy—not easy to find a princess in her vast residence. I follow the large entrance-hall on the left—go up, down, get lost, come out in the Chapel of the Holy Shroud, go up the black marble steps into the Sala degli Svizzeri, through the Sala degli Staffieri, the Sala dei Paggi, the Throne Room, the Audience Chamber, the Chamber of the Grand Council. Ladies and gentlemen—the most esteemed names of subalpine nobility—those who today survive only in paintings—they come, go, laugh, and talk with lips of flesh . . .

But *La Bela Madamin*? Where is she? Where is the delicate ghost of my hallucinations? I walk through the long Galleria del Danieli, under the fabulous skies of some seventeen-century painter, continue forward amidst the sparkling crystal of immense chandeliers, open a door that is ajar. I hear a voice. *La Bela Madamin*. No. It's not her. I become pale.

In the middle of the room, leaning on a work table with his arms folded, is His Majesty King Victor Amadeus III, already in gala attire, resembling to a remarkable degree the portrait of Dogliotti,[1] as seen in Rinaudi's engraving, his rigid profile not in the least softened by his white wig, collar of the Annunziata, ribbons, crosses and medals carefully arranged on the exceedingly shiny breastplate of that peaceful eighteenth-century warrior, the purple with the white cross of the imperial mantel and wrapped with a Roman line, relaxed somewhat by the graces of Watteau.

His Majesty is re-reading a letter; the parchment flutters between his nervous thumbs, moved by his trembling. And he doesn't listen to Count Lamarmora who is reading to him the well-planned formalities of the excursion in official protocol, which will later be put in the State Archives according to court custom, decreeing:

". . . from Vercelli to Milan, from Milan to Roveredo to Innsbruck, where we expect to arrive next Saturday. In the retinue of Duchess Carolina there will be the Marquis of Bianzè, her first Equerry and Knight of Honour; Magistrate Borsetti, Secretary of State; the Marquise of Cinzano, Lady in Waiting; the Countess of Salmour and the Marquise of Verolengo, Ladies of the Palace . . ."

"*E souma inteis, e souma inteis*,"[2] the King interrupts, with a gesture that silences Count Lamarmora, and he dis-

---

1 Orazio Dogliotti (1832 - 1892), an Italian general and writer.
2 Turinese dialect: "We have agreed, we have agreed."

charges him, saying: "*Ca fassa chiel; ma dsôura a tüt gnüne masnôiade, gnün tapage an facia a la pôpôlassiôn . . .*"[1]

Oh, my sweet dialect so alive amongst so many dead things, which I love more than any other language, more than Italian (which I truly love!)—Italian, which is alien to my subalpine inner core, learned late with great love and great effort like a language that is not my own. But my sweet Turinese is the only language in which I think and the only one that reaches my heart, sincerely provoking smiles and tears—my sweet Turinese on the lips of a King of Savoy, when Piedmont was still a charming province of France, and Italy had not yet come into being—I cannot describe the emotions felt by this!

"*E souma inteis,*" His Majesty concludes, without raising his eyes from the letter.

And the letter was from Anton Clemens, Duke of Saxony, the distant son-in-law—the unknown gentleman who is waiting in a barbaric land for the gentle young woman. It says: "*. . . Il en coûtera sans doute à la sensibilité de Madame la Princesse de s'éloigner de ses illustres parents et d'une famille qui doit lui être chère, mais je mettrai tant d'attention à faire diversion à ses soucis et à m'attirer sa confiance et son estime que je me flatte de lui adoucir l'amertume de cette separation . . .*"[2]

---

1 "Turinese dialect: You take care of the matter; but the important thing is that we don't have any childish behaviour—no scene before the people . . ."

2 French: ". . . Without doubt it will cost the sensibility of Madame the Princess a great deal to leave her illustrious parents and family, who must be very dear the her, but I will dedicate much attention toward reversing her sorrows and gaining her trust and esteem and shall be proud to sweeten the bitterness of this separation . . ."

✳

But *La Bela Madamin?*

I walk into the Chinese Room, then through the rooms of blue, crimson, strawberry, canary, and willow-coloured satin, to the apartment of the Queen, pausing in the Persian corridor to listen to the comments of two ladies: "Adorable! Adorable!"

They are talking about her—so she must be nearby. Now I am in the Cabinet of Miniatures in the Pompeian Gallery—a pungent perfume tells me that I have penetrated the sanctuary of that hidden flower. And on the threshold I pause, dazzled before of the most delicate living interpretation ever done of *La toilette de la Mariée.*[1]

Maria Carolina Antonietta of Savoy, the Duchess of Saxony, is standing between her maids, some bending over her, some on their knees, intent on their delicate work. Her sister-in-law, who presides over the process with Parisian expertise, takes the mirror from her hand:

"You can look at yourself later, *mignonne, quand le rêve sera achevé.*"[2]

Maria Carolina is a dazzling vision of snow and sliver.

A white tuft of feathers adorning a tall, powered coiffure; a white face passed over with white ceruse; a shiny satin dress with a monstrous hoop skirt; white shoes, garlands, a dog and a fan. The red of her lips and cheeks, the black of her eyes and eyebrows, stand out against

---

1 The attire of the bride.
2 "You can look at yourself later, darling, when the dream has been completed."

such whiteness. Her sister-in-law, Adélaïde of France, the niece of Louis XV,[1] has painted the face of the eighteen-year-old child according to the latest dictates of Parisian fashion—with cosmetics she has erased her delicate blonde eyebrows and painted two others, black, arched, and imperious, in the middle of her forehead, to take their place.

Her hairstyle had been discussed at length. De Regault, the court hairdresser, had wanted, with that immense head of blonde hair, to reproduce the Palazzo Madama or the Capitan Galley of the Sardinian States, but the Queen and Princess disagreed and the artist instead with that thick foliage constructed a three-tiered edifice crowned with a nest in which a dove, assisted by her companion, tenderly broods.

"*Ravissante! Ravissante!*"[2] murmurs the sister-in-law who stands behind her, adjusting with her own hand now a flower, now a fold in the hoop skirt.

But suddenly, seeing the graceful adolescent shoulders shaking, she bends over and looks—that face, painted with such care, is flooded with tears.

"*Ah, mon Dieu, tu va te ravager!*[3] But really! Come, come and look at yourself, and don't cry anymore."

She takes the bride by the hand, guiding her before a huge oval mirror on the wall. The tears suddenly stop. The child, who yesterday still played with the visiting ladies, is dismayed to be today an actual lady herself

---

1 Gozzano is mistaken. Adélaïde was the daughter of Louis XV. Her and her sister visited Turin in 1791.
2 "Ravishing! Ravishing!"
3 "Oh, my God, you are destroying yourself!"

and did not imagine she would see herself so beautiful. Amidst her fading sobs she smiles—smiles at herself, her sister-in-law, the maids, erasing the last trace of her tears with a powder puff.

"Her Majesty the Queen!" a servant announces.

Valets, hairdressers, servants, spring to their feet, rigid against the wall.

The mother pauses at the door, smiles and stretches her arms out toward her daughter—embracing, kissing her, but with anxious delicacy, as if breathing in the smell of a too fragile flower.

"*Un rêve, vraiment un rêve!*"[1]

> *Da già che a l'è cusì, da già ch'à l'è destin,*
> *faruma la girada anturn a tüt Türin.*

Oh, the endless line of carriages—the carriages of the Royal House which are like tall up-side-down triangles, engraved, gilded, overburdened with all the mythology and mad symbolism of the baroque—so clumsy and graceful, slender and stumpy all at once!

Berlins of four, six, ten horses with caparisons, fringes, plumes—with nothing left free but the legs and abundant tail; coachmen and footmen with stiff ponytails like automatons taken from a hundred-year-old closet! . . .

The fantastic procession goes on interminably, like in one of Perrault's fairy tales, but without the Marquis of Carabattole, or the Cat in Boots, or Cinderella become queen, having instead all the ladies of subalpine nobility—the Marchioness of San Damiano, the Marchioness

---

1 "A dream, truly a dream!"

146

of Ormea, Countess Morozzo, Countess Della Rocca, the Marchioness of Saint-Germain, the Marchioness of Cinzano, the Countess of Salmour, the Marchioness of Verolengo. . . .

And amidst all of these is the bride, all in white, silver—exquisite, like the Princess of the fairy tale, like the daughter of the King—legendary . . .

—*La Bela Carôlin!*

The crowd throngs the Piazza Castello, the arcades, the colonnades, buzzing in the trees, on the fences, roofs, cheering the bride with heartfelt joy. The people love the last-born of the King, love her like a small and delicate little child—*La Bela Carôlin* is popular everywhere, from the park of the Venaria to that of Valentino, from the ramparts of the Citadel to the ramparts of the Dora, where she doesn't disdain to interrupt her diversion to speak to a gardener who prunes, to a laundress shedding tears.

—*Madama Carôlin! La Bela Carôlin!*

Never have the people felt their tenderness moved to such a degree as now, at the time of this last farewell. The beautiful flower of Savoy will soon be picked by other hands in a garden beyond the Alps.

> *Da già che a l'è cusì, da già ch'à l'è destin,*
> *faruma la girada anturn a tüt Türin.*

The long parade of equipages passes along the Via Dora Grossa to the Porta Segusina, and goes from the Porta Segusina to the ramparts of the Cittadella. There, all the troops are deployed—the Granatieri and the

Guastatori in their scarlet uniforms trimmed with silver, their fringed hats with the bands also inlaid with silver and blue stand out—as does the Compagnia Colonnella and the Guild of Merchants and Grocers in their most lively uniforms. Along the Via Santa Teresa and through the Piazza San Carlo, along the Via Nuova—beneath all the other personnel of the city—the Students of the Royal University and their Mayors, the Knights of the Order of SS. Annunziata and of the Order of Maurice and Lazarus. All of them form amidst the crowd an orderly pattern of bright colours, the procession passing between them as between a double hedge of dazzling uniforms.

The seventeen-year-old bride has never seen so much splendour in her short and cosy life and, realizing that all that joy of colour and sound is for her, stands up and claps her hands as if she were playing a delightful game. From the bastions of the Cittadella to the bastions of the Po, the cannons rumble, the mortars and the firecrackers cry out, incessantly accompanying with a militant roar the exultant clanging of all the bells of all the churches—the Metropolitana, Santa Teresa, the Consolata, the Santi Martiri Tebei, and all the provincial temples of Turin.

The royal procession advances. Ladies and knights continuously throw out handfuls of wedding *dragées*, and those large eighteenth-century candies called *giüraje*. And the crowd throngs about, waving, cheering. The bride stretches out her hands and a thousand others reach out in an affectionate grasp of final farewell.

—*La Bela Carôlin!*

The Piazza San Carlo has been turned into an immense room: "there is a table on which can be seen a series of bowls filled with white candies and various types of sugared pastries and fruits, very much out of season. These bowls, with their contents piled high in pyramids on the top of which banners bearing coats of arms and figures display themselves, the whole presented with pyramids of flowers supported by four silver bulls loaded with candies. In the end, their Royal Highnesses receive more pleasure from their eyes than their mouths, as they watch the table being plundered and the pyramids of fruit and sugar climbed upon."

The young bride laughs at this game—laughs at the crowd as it runs, climbs, rolls and makes noise, until tears run down her cheeks. The bride has forgotten all else and thinks that her life is nothing but a gilded and flower-decked procession amidst a multitude of gay and cheering people. For her, the joy of the occasion is like the honey placed on the rim of a glass of bitter medicine.

The crowd stretches from outside the Porta Nuova to Valentino Park. In front of the castle, in the area called the "Ladies' Diversion," the procession stops once again for another refreshment and to receive the compliments of the poet Pancrazio da Bra, a well-known Arcadian at the Accademia degli Incolti.

He moves forward, dressed as the River Po, half-naked, with a mantle of golden cloth and his hair in the guise of seaweed, and is followed by Dora, a girl dressed like a nymph with dishevelled hair. They begin a dialogue in verse in which the Po demonstrates to Dora, disconsolate at the departure of the Princess, how the House of Savoy extending its splendour beyond all borders is a necessity . . .

Our sky deprives itself of such a beautiful star!

La Bela Carôlin, bored to death by the endless academic poem, yawns, grows glum, looks away, gets up impatiently—is restrained in vain by her mother and sister-in-law.

Once again she feels the bitterness of the coming separation, the reality of the sad occasion, and her distracted heart is constricted for a short while. . . . Her face becomes veiled with anguish when the procession goes once more through the Porta di Po.

There, under the arcades decked out in flags and flowers, the four travelling carriages in which she would have to soon leave are waiting—not gracious gilded carriages, but instead giant coaches, dark and unadorned.

The procession comes to a halt near the city gates. She has to, with the Marquise of Cinzano, the Countess of Salmour, the Marquis of Bianzé, leave the carriage in which she sits—has to with these travelling companions, get into the sad, no longer gala vehicles. The short walk is indicated by a carpet strewn with flowers . . .

But *La Bela Carôlin,* who has been squeezing the hand of the Queen for the last half hour, now clings to her arm, and when Count Lamarmora opens the door and invites her to descend, the little one throws herself on her mother's neck, desperate, crazy.

Her brother is compelled to undo her arms by force as if he were breaking a chain—by force they make her step out, make her walk the short distance that is junketed with flowers, holding her by the shoulders, forcing her to move on, nearly lifting her up bodily into the travelling coach. And within, the child sees that she is lost.

"*Maman! Maman!*" she shouts, leaning out of the window while the four carriages part the crowd. "*Maman! Maman!*"

Alas, her mother and friends remain behind, to return in the gilded carriages to the Royal Palace she has had to leave forever. So the little one is seized by a mad panic as if she were being dragged to her death. Before her are the severe Marquise of Salmour and the grim Ambassador of Saxony. She sees that she is alone, lost, and frantically leans toward the crowd to beg for help.

"*Maman! Maman!*"

And the mothers in the crowd have heard her—many women push themselves around the wheels, almost preventing the carriages from going forward, pressing the girl's small, trembling hands.

"*Povra masnà!*"

"*Che Dio at giüta!*"

"*Fate courâge!*"

"*Arvëdse ancoura!*"

"*Arvëdse prest!*"[1]

But the coachmen whip the horses—the convoy gains speed, cutting through the crowd, goes off at a gallop—is on the bridge, beyond the river, disappears . . .

---

1 "Poor girl!"
"May God help you!"
"Be brave!"
"See you again!"
"See you soon!"

The Duke of Saxony was an excellent spouse for *La Bela Carôlin.*

On March 17th he wrote to the Queen, thanking her for giving her consent and for the happiness which followed.

"Aussi tous mes désirs ne tendront-ils qu'à me rendre digne des bontés d'une princesse qui réunit aux charmes de la plus aimable figure, toutes les vertus de ses augustes parents."[1]

On December 28th, 1782 *La Bela Carôlin* died in Dresden, a little more than a year after her marriage, having not yet reached nineteen years of age.

Tuchè-me'n po' la man, me cari sitadin,
Për vive che mi viva vëdrö pi Türin!

---

1 French: "So now all my desires will go toward proving myself worthy of the goodness of a princess who unites the charms of the most amiable face with all the virtues of her royal parents."

Alcina

"**Y**OU are a materialist."

"No, absolutely not!"

"You are. You say that you're not only for the sake of modishness, to be chic, because materialism is no longer in fashion, but these days all of you intellectuals and thinkers are materialists acting as if your senses were more refined and you were more sophisticated. That is why you are more tedious, less happy, and more false!"

Once again, Miss Eleanor Quarrell had assaulted me with her somewhat rough directness, but in her voice I noticed an affectionate pity which told me how much she cared for me and how unhappy I must have seemed to her.

The little hunchback was staring at me with sweet, inquiring eyes in which, now and again, the blue irises, as if following the rhythm of her thoughts, were devoured by velvet-coloured pupils. Those eyes, that perfect profile, that saintly, suffering smile recalled the divine head of a martyr cut off and set on a body that was not its own, condemned like Rigoletto[1] to a double gibbosity. She was

---

1 The hunchbacked court jester from Giuseppe Verdi's opera of the same name.

secured with resigned dignity inside her perpetual, conventual tunic. The only distinction of noble richness on this grey cloth, which enveloped her like a hairshirt, was a massive antique gold chain studded with large gems: a piece of jewellery of almost barbaric making, passed down from mother to daughter, and worn by all the blonde great-grandmothers who had been sleeping for centuries in the crypts of their family abbey, over there, in far-away Devonshire.

For many years Miss Eleanor had been wintering in Sicily, not returning to her vast and foggy country until late spring. Her father, a number of years earlier, had passed away on the hill which overlooked Girgenti,[1] and the deformed young lady devoted herself to that sky and ocean, against which the most intact examples of Italo-Greek art were silhouetted as if against two different types of cobalt. The well-known temples had been the passion and glory of the illustrious archaeologist, and possibly the cause of his premature death. Lord Quarrell had belonged to that group of devoted and fervent Englishmen who, electing Magna Graecia as their ideal homeland, united their efforts and names to those of the most enlightened Italian connoisseurs. He had been responsible for the unearthing of two of the most beautiful metopes of Selinunte: Minerva killing a giant, and Diana splashing Actaeon. He also definitively mapped out the structure of the entire Temple of Demeter, and reconstituted one of

______

1 The Sicilian name for Agrigento. The name was used until 1929 when, under fascist rule, the Italianised "Agrigento," the name used by the ancient Romans, was imposed. In this story Gozzano uses both names.

the Atlases which had been broken, the pieces scattered about—a sculpture which supported the architrave of the Temple of Hercules.

Left alone, the deformed young lady devoted herself to that sacred region. In the hills, facing the famous temples, amongst olive and orange trees, she built the Buona Sosta: the Good Rest-House—a bizarre yet modest structure for a woman who had perfect taste in art and owned an Elizabethan castle and an entire province in England. A bungalow of elementary simplicity, completely white, with only a single story, exposed to the entire horizon by immense windows. Inside, there was a refined absence of any particular style: white walls, floors and ceiling; clean wood and enamel, very little furniture, no knick-knacks; only a single elegant touch: flowers and plants of all sorts and, through the large windows, a view of the sky, ocean, and temples.

And yet the little white house emanated the fascination of a palace, just as the little deformed person did a mysterious power. Miss Eleanor was truly the first woman I had ever encountered who had *consciousness* and *intelligence*. I was irresistibly attracted to the serenity that radiated from that miserable being, that vehement faith near which the soul warmed itself as if by a spiritual flame—she was a source of inexhaustible consolation.

"You know the art of being happy."

"It's easy. You only have to forget yourself in the happiness of others."

"I don't care for humanity. I don't love my neighbour."

"But they and you are the same. The soul . . ."

"You know that I don't believe in the soul!"

"It isn't true. You believe, because you suffer by not believing. How can one not believe in the only thing that is certain, in the only truth we have within us, which is more certain than any physical reality, more obvious than—let me see—than the Earth being round, than the infinity of space? Why are you laughing? No, do not laugh, my dear! I'm not espousing theosophy. I know that you detest it. I would simply like to share with you things that do me good! Let us reason." Miss Eleanor took my hands, held them in hers, and looked at me with intense tenderness. "Let us reason about it, you who love plain thinking. Here, today, our hands are clinging together. They will not be the same hands which will meet in six or seven years. This is something even vulgar science agrees with. They will be other hands, transformed down to their tiniest particles. Our entire bodies will be transformed. Our two personas will move toward each other, calling each other by name, smiling, and they will be two strangers meeting for the first time. And yet, isn't it true that we will meet with the same effusion? We will recognise each other with joy, and we will always be us. Our friendship will be unchanged and we shall talk of the past, talk of days long gone as if they were things of the present. There is, therefore, beneath the appearance of a body that changes a thing that does not change, a spiritual element that registers the changes, of miserable matter. How can you not believe in this present witness?"[1]

---

1 She is speaking of Advaita Vedanta. It is likely, however, that Gozzano was reading Madame Blavatsky rather than any original Indian sources.

I had been in Girgenti for almost a month and every day climbed up to the Buona Sosta to listen to my friend speak of these singular things. I had returned from a long trip in the East, freeing myself from its discomforts and climates, but, altered by the shameful habit of hypnotics,[1] had chosen to stay there for a period before going back to Piedmont, in part due to the advice of Dr. Gaudenzi, my dear Sicilian friend, who observed that, after wandering through Japan and Papua New Guinea, an Italian might also visit Italy.

So, for a month I had been living there, in the enchantment of Magna Greca, in Girgenti, amongst the ruins of ancient Acragante, *the fairest of mortal cities*,[2] the birthplace of Theron[3] and Empedocles, feeling at heart ashamed to have lived almost thirty years in ignorance of the glory of our sky.

I visited the Buona Sosta every day. Miss Eleanor's conversation was enchanting. She spoke Italian with the somewhat overly literary correctness of a foreigner who has studied our language deeply; but her slightly exotic accent, which was not really incorrect, lent such a gracefulness to her speech that I often simply enjoyed her voice without following the meaning of her words.

"The thing that does not change! The witness! . . . Dear, dear Eleanor, I think that, despite all your goodwill, you cannot do a thing for me. Faith is not acquired through reason. It comes by grace."

---

1 Probably opium.

2 A quote from Pindar's *Twelfth Pythian Ode*. The English rendering used here is borrowed from a translation by the Reverend C.A. Wheelright.

3 Theron of Acragas (died 473 BC), was a Sicilian tyrant.

"Faith," my friend sighed, casting her glance over the scenery of colossal stones that stood before us. "Faith is what moves boulders, and makes everything, absolutely everything, possible."

"Everything?" I asked myself, and instinctively, without turning to look at her, thought of her miserable body, humped and only as high as a stool, an atrocious prank of wicked nature.

And Eleanor, in a calm voice, replied immediately to my silence:

"Everything is possible. Yes, even this."

We were in the atrium, which was completely cloaked in maidenhair moss. In front of us was the scenery I had been enjoying for the past month, and which each day I felt as if I were seeing for the first time. A green slope of orange trees, speckled with golden fruit, then the blue of the ocean, the blue of the sky; and on that horizon of three different enamels, the most divine representations that Doric art has, together with the Parthenon, ever handed down to us. The Temple of Concord, and, nearby, the Temple of Hera with its parade of twenty erect columns and twenty fallen, and, further on, the Temple of Hercules, a frightening ossuary of Carthaginic barbarity, a wonder so cyclopean that our imagination, instead of asking how it was built, asks only how it was destroyed; and further on still, the Temple of Olympian Zeus, the Temple of Castor and Pollux: all the sacred ruins with which Agrigento challenged the blue of the sky and of the sea: hecatombs of granite and marble which seemed to cover the entire earth with columns, severed or lying, capitals, cubes, plates, divine fragments.

But in front of us stood the Temple of Demeter, the temple that Miss Eleanor called "her temple." It stood with its fifty-four columns, intact amidst ten others that had collapsed, the only one which had, by some strange privilege, survived the fury of the Phoenicians and Carthaginians, the fanaticism of the Christians and Saracens.

"No, my friend. That the temple is still intact is due to the Christians and Saracens. Saint Ronald, in the fourth century, selected it to be among the 'infernal monuments of idolatry' and converted it into a church dedicated to Saint John the Evangelist. Later, during the Saracen invasion, the church was transformed into a mosque. And the divine monument was saved, hidden and protected in an encasing of stone and cement like a fossil. Such is the kindness of chance! Consider the ruin caused by the others! I will publish one of my father's manuscripts which is dedicated to the study of these nefarious destructions. Think of the colossal Temple of Hercules that provided material for all the Medieval harbours! Everything was smashed and destroyed. The cyclopean columns, each flute of which could have held a man as if inside a niche, were pulled down, as were the giants and twelve-metre-tall Sybilles that supported the architrave—marvels of titanic mass and perfect sculpting. Think of the heads, arms, divine shoulders, and capitals around which they secured gigantic hawsers, pulled and stretched taut by whipped oxen, while saws cut and spades undermined the masterpieces at their bases. And the enormous building crashed into frightening pieces, with a roar that shook the earth. Now, on that divine nudity, between the folds of peploses, the sea anemones and octopuses of Porto Empedocle make their nests."

"Things to invoke a second bull of Phalaris[1] for Christian vandals."

"The flock! The flock of the Abbey!" Miss Eleanor, with a childish impulse, cried out abruptly. "The flock of the Abbey! How charming!"

Suddenly, from inside the Temple, two or three hundred snow-coloured sheep appeared against the grey of the huge columns. They were coming out after their afternoon rest, out from the cool shade, running along the portico, leaping on the plinths, descending with a great bleating and tinkling of bells.

Three shepherds, with their dogs, were busy gathering in the slower ones and those which went astray. A few, the smallest, did not dare to jump from the high granite cubes, but ran desperately along the portico, stretching their necks and, with a plaintive bleating, calling for help. The shepherds took them in their arms and passed them from one to the next, amidst the barking of dogs.

"I do not regret being born too late. The picture is more divine now than in the days of Empedocle. The sky,

---

1 Phalaris was a tyrant of Agrigento. He had a bronze bull constructed which he used as a device of torture, putting his victims within and cooking them there until they bellowed.

seen through columns of overly vivid stucco, must have seemed less blue. I cannot imagine the metopes, triglyphs, and listels painted yellow, blue, and green. I can only think of them in the colour of granite, the colour of time, as seen through the melancholy present. With its plinths and streaks of columns painted, adorned and decorated—its precisely measured pediments not yet softened by millenniums—immense banners waving in the wind and a crowd that poured in on solemn days— the temple had to have been less beautiful than today. Today, it has a beauty that appeals to me, a beauty that agonises!"

"Your hotel is also rather agonizing," my friend interrupted with a laugh. "I see that it has yet another *réclame.*"

Below, at the foot of Girgenti, shoved against its slope like some pitiable heiress, shimmered the immense cube of the Hotel d'Agrigento. On its white walls and the walls of its park, which stretched up to the hundred-year-old cypress trees, the praises of tonic beverages and aperitifs stood out in colossal lettering.

"And what are they doing at the hotel?"

"I forgot to tell you. They are preparing a concert for Nino Karavetzky, the nine-year-old prodigy. Tomorrow evening, during the full moon, he will play at the Temple."

"They do such things every year," Eleanor said, her face clouding over. "Last year, the colony of foreigners organised a pleasant gathering. Venetian lanterns were hung between the columns. There were rockets, Bengal lights, dances, and *The Merry Widow*."[1]

---

1 A popular comedy operetta by composer Franz Lehár.

"This year, the idea is less outrageous."

"I was only joking. I know the young Karavetzky and heard him last summer at the Conservatory of Brussels. He is more than an *enfant prodige*. He is one who reveals. I will be happy to hear him again."

"Oh! What a pleasure! Then you will come!"

"I will not go, but will listen from here. I will be able to hear the sound of the violin and not the comments of the Raineri girls and Madame Delassaux."

I was genuinely distressed by this resolute refusal. I tried to coax my friend, holding out the programme to her.

"Look, look how delightful it will be."

She looked it over, commenting like a connoisseur.

"Delightful, but I still will not go."

"Oh, dear Eleanor, how your refusal saddens me. When they told me about the concert I immediately thought of you—the pleasure of sitting apart with you, on some broken capital, and listening to the distant music and the things that you alone understand of our buried beauty."

"And, well-illuminated by the full moon, watched over by Madame Delassaux or someone else on her behalf, for another fairy-tale to be weaved *sur la sorcière des ruines*.[1] No, do not protest, you know very well that they call me this."

I did not reply, but, bending forward, pressed my burning cheeks against her hands, which were cold and delicate.

---

1 . . . about the witch of the ruins.

"My poor friend," she said, "as long as we are among the living, the world will do as it pleases."

I was silent at first, but then spoke without lifting my face.

"I am very disappointed. I was counting on your presence. I'm a vagabond without a soul who neither believes nor feels. But, next to you, I seem to feel and believe in something. I don't know—I don't know how to explain what I feel when I'm near you."

Eleanor slowly withdrew her hands. Lifting up my face, I saw the change on hers, and in her eyes, where the blue irises were devoured by velvet-coloured pupils that scrutinised me to the depths of my soul.

"It is true. You are sincere," said Eleanor in a voice that was at once emotional and firm. "Since we feel affection for each other, I will go. Wait for me near the fourth metope; I promise that during the *Notturno* of Sinding, I will be with you. My soul," she corrected herself, "will be there with you!"

Disappointed and dissatisfied, I smiled bitterly at the game she was playing with her words. But Eleanor, without smiling, raised her hand as if she were taking a vow.

"I will be with you."

And even as I turned to say goodbye from the doorway, with that smile of disbelief and disappointment on my lips, she repeated solemnly:

"I swear that I will be with you!"

Why did that promise and that almost tragic expression of tenderness make me shiver? I left the Buona Sosta in a strange state of excitement, setting out almost at a run toward the hotel. Halfway there, Dr. Gaudenzi sprang out from the shade of a stand of agave and cactus.

"Finally I get a chance to see you! You spend every day at the Buona Sosta. From the ruins to the hunchback, from the hunchback to the ruins. There is not much difference. I'm starting to regret having introduced her to you. For many reasons."

"Let's hear it."

"You came here to put your nerves back in order and the company of that dreamer is the very opposite of a remedy. I have known her for years and would bet that you have been talking with her all day long about art and the afterlife, which are her specialties. Your eyes look rather glassy."

"And you? What better things have you done?"

"We went to Porto Empedocle to see the nets pulled in. We helped the fishermen and sailors, a work-out that would have been beneficial to you as well. Then, along with the ladies, we invaded a tavern in the lower harbour and ate fried fish *alla saracena,* after which we made a bet on who could run more times around the fountain of San Rocco while carrying Madame Delassaux between their arms. She weighs ninety-six kilos. I won second prize . . ."

My friend was right. My mistake, however, was in choosing for relaxation a land where every stone had a magic power, a fabulous past, was intoxicating and hallucinatory. Liguria would have been better, the only beautiful things there being the orange and olive trees, or better still my own Canavese,[1] which lacked any kind of brilliant past, but was still green with refreshing peace, and where one could be at ease like a good bourgeois.

"I will visit Miss Eleanor less frequently. You are right. Her conversation fascinates me."

"You'd better. And not only for your nerves. There is a lot of murmuring about your assiduity. Today I heard a perverse sentence about the romance '*du poète languissant e la bossue aux soixante millions.*'[2] No, you can't slap anyone on the face because the person who said it was a woman. Only women are capable of thinking these kinds of things. But women say them and men believe and repeat them."

The Temple of Demeter was tinted silver by the full moon! A beauty that no type of art could reproduce without having recourse to some common oleograph—a beauty only tolerable in hard reality. But what a reality! The land, the ocean, the sky of Agrigento were fused together in a neutral tint, the uncoloured scenery seeming to give precedence to that unique form—and the temple lifted itself onto its five-stepped stereobate, its precise columns, rigid, converging from the plinths to the capitals with a harmony that was like a prayer hurled upward, toward the absolute. On this symphony of seven by seven, of the twenty by twenty columns of the architrave, the triangles

---

1 In Northern Italy. This was in fact the region that Gozzano was from.

2 "the languishing poet and the hunchback worth sixty million."

of the balanced pediments were like two stanzas in full profile against the moon, the moonlight rejuvenating the temple as a stage makes the face of a woman young again.

"Man was able to do this! This cry for the ideal he solidified into stone."

My excitement grew. I wandered through the crowd with unsteady steps. It pressed forward, spectators coming in from all sides, both Italians and foreigners—but these modern figures, minuscule on the impressive steps, between the colossal intercolumnations, did not break the harmony of the picture, as our changeable fashions were simply pitiful against that beauty that never changes.

Inside, between the double colonnades of the cella, before the three worn-out altars, the spectators gathered. The women stopped chattering and the men took off their hats as they entered, instinctively, as if the deity was still present.

"Eleanor! Eleanor!" What was my friend doing at the Buona Sosta amidst the maidenhair fern? Why wasn't she with me at that divine hour?

The full moon lit up everything almost as if it were daylight, making the eyes, teeth and jewellery of the ladies sparkle; some of them—those who were year-round residents—wore hats, low-necked dresses, and light-coloured shoes or brightly-coloured gold and silver lamé; other ladies—the foreigners—were dressed in the scanty outfits of travellers.

And, between the parting wings of the crowd, the little wizard appeared, led forward by his mother, a still young and beautiful woman. How tiny the famous prodigy was! A murmur of tender surprise was transformed into amiable laughter when the little fellow tried two or three times, in vain, to climb onto the plinth, and his mother lifted him up and put him down with a kiss and a smile, offering him the instrument in its open case like a favourite toy. The boy picked it up as if it were an old wooden horse he was going to play with and, holding it between his bare legs, rapping on it with his knuckles, pinching the strings with his fingers and nibbling at them with his teeth, tuned it.

Leaning against a column, I watched him through the crowd, a minute Mozart on his Greek plinth, and my uneasiness increased. I could feel blood rumbling through my head which was pressed against the granite. My eyes ached and, if I closed them, the edges of their lids burned as if they were made of red-hot metal. I waited for the music in the same way that, during desperate nights, I asked my friend for the drug of oblivion or the pitiful injection.

The first delightful note—it was Max Bruch's Concerto in D minor—scratched itself into my brain. The great miracle brought about by the young interpreter, from the vigorously passionate sonority of the first phrases to the gleeful, leaping finale, was for me a nameless martyrdom, like listening to some diabolical music played on a crystal slab with a diamond bow by a demon.

"Eleanor! Eleanor!"

What was my friend doing then? Was she listening, her poor deformed person throbbing under the maidenhair fern of the Buona Sosta?

I did not see the crowd, but only her. The notes transformed themselves into her words: ". . . faith, faith that makes everything possible: this too!" Lowering her eyes indicating the misfortune of her miserable body, then lifting the blue irises: ". . . I will come! Make sure you can see me. My soul will be there with you. I swear that I will come!"

Trembling with excitement, I looked around for the doctor, as for a saviour, without being able to find him. I looked for a capital, some stone on which I could sit, but they were all were taken up by the ladies. My knees could no longer support me. I walked around the column, passed through the intercolumns of the cella to the external intercolumns, beneath the full light of the moon.

I almost ran along the portico to get away from the malefic sounds and feel the coolness of the evening fan my face. When I reached the fourth metope, I walked down two or three steps and leaned against the granite, my head supported by an incline in the worn out stone.

Before me was colourless land and colourless sea, only visible due to the tremulous reflections of the moon. On one side, oblique, was the sarcophagus of Phaedra, the figures on it made more visible by the slanting light. For a few seconds I forgot my misery. The queen was seated, with one stiff arm leaning on a stool, the other left limp in the hands of two female slaves who caressed it, anxiously, with sorrow. . . . The woman's inconsolable profile, in which was condensed all human desperation, the blameless desperation of being what we are, of not being able to be other than what we are, was turned away. Love—a tiny Love that was like a little demon—was there on one side, grinning, contemplating the effect of its arrow. But the other demon, the little demon of our day, the Magician of Sounds who, even there, persecuted me with the divine martyrdom of his instrument! Even Sarasate's[1] gay and springy *Zingaresca* did not offer relief. I caressed the folds of the neat, thrice-millenarian tunic.

"Grief—here, too, there is grief, immortalised in hard stone!"

Wanting to lose myself forever in some dead thing, in something that no longer suffered, that would never again suffer, I looked up at the moon.

"Eleanor! Eleanor!"

Ah! Why did I not have her near me? Why had she not agreed to meet me?

I stared at the sky for a long time. For too long. When I lowered my eyes I saw the lunar disk multiplying itself in red wherever I looked. I closed my eyes, pressing my fingers against them for a while in order to erase the image of the bloody disc from my inner eyelids. Sinding's *Chanson triste*, the favourite nocturne of Eleanor, reached out through the silence. Was her soul really close? Certainly, her soul could also hear it from her flower-covered veranda, but she wasn't suffering like me! My very unhappy friend knew the secret of happiness!

In the distance, the young performer multiplied his improvised effects and the music was so very close to me that the strings seemed to vibrate in my ears. But I heard a light step along the porch. The annoying person halted two or three times behind me, with a rustling that seemed to be in time with the rhythm of the music. I

---

1 Pablo de Serasate, a renowned Spanish violinist and composer.

didn't want to lift my face from my hands, and didn't lift it even when I heard the stranger come down and sit beside me.

With my head down, I looked, from bottom to top, and saw two minuscule feet, perfectly fitted in jewelled buskins, then a smart tunic gathered together at the knees like a half-closed fan. It was wrapped gracefully around a perfect bust, enveloping slender shoulders, leaving the neck and the face as in a wimple, leaving only the profile uncovered, the profile of Eleanor.

I didn't jump, or even give a cry. I tried to convince myself that I was not dreaming by touching the granite and biting my lips to feel the cold and pain. I was not dreaming.

"You are not dreaming! You are not dreaming!"

Eleanor spoke! I couldn't say how her voice sounded—perhaps the syllables of her words and the notes coming from afar were the same thing. But she spoke, standing upright before me, and I could not find the strength to jump to my feet. She stretched out both hands, weaving her soft fingers between mine. Her person was absolute, the word beauty being too human to describe the divine revelation which stood before me, that soul turned to flesh in a form copied from the immortal statues.

"You are not dreaming! You are not dreaming! I made a promise. I came."

"No, it isn't true!" I held her fingers tightly. "I'll wake up soon and everything will be as if it had never happened and I will not have these hands of yours, I will only have my nails stuck in my bloody palms. I understand the deception of dreams."

"You are not dreaming! Oh, why this childish pride when confronted by mystery? Why do you rebel against yourself? You called for me as for everything divine. I came. And I came the way I want to be. Anything is possible. This too."

"Eleanor! Eleanor! What if this is only a momentary truth before the coming of endless darkness?"

"The light will come. The time has come. For years I have waited for you. A miracle has been performed!"

"Eleanor, if this is not a dream," and I leaped to my feet and held her thin waist, "then let me take you among men, crying your name out loud in the world of the living!"

And I tried to drag the warm, throbbing form across the portico, toward the interior of the temple.

"No, no! Faith alone has performed this miracle. Do not profane the mystery!"

She resisted and I grasped her around the waist, determined to drag the divine dream into reality, quite certain that with the last note everything would vanish into thin air. And I did not want this. I wanted to snatch the divine form from the powers of the occult.

"No! Be careful! Don't profane the mystery! Faith alone has done this! You will lose me forever! Let me go! Let me go!"

It was a determined resistance, a hostile fight for the supreme good.

"Let me go! Let me go!"

I lifted her and she resisted, shaking as if I was carrying her to death; then, with a scream, she went limp, falling back insensible. I carried her between the intercolumns, triumphing to have gone from dream to reality with that significant prey, to lift her up before all, crying out that it was a miracle.

But it was then that things started to seem like a dream.

For a moment I saw the crowd gathered and the little musician playing on the plinth. Then nothing more. And in the dark, a scream, many screams; and the lunar disc was painted again in my wandering mind in blood and then a real voice, the voice of Madame Delassaux, my enemy.

"*Il est ivre, il est fou! Par ici, sauvez-vous par ici, Miss Quarrell!*"[1]

Then nothing more. The absence of time and space. The happiness of not being.

✳

And after a time, though how long I do not know, I saw through half-closed eyelids a rolling meadow dotted with unearthly flowers, similar to those drawn by occultists when depicting the landscapes of Jupiter and Saturn, and I felt a chill, a chill that was at contrast with the marvellous flora.

I opened my very real eyes to the very real light, seeing that the bright field was the cover of my bed altered due to my reclining perspective, and realised that the chill came from an icepack that covered my temples. I lifted my hand to my forehead, but Dr. Gaudenzi stopped me

---

1 "He is drunk, mad! Come this way and save yourself Miss Quarrell!"

and smiled, speaking in an affectionate and calm manner, as if resuming a conversation interrupted half an hour before.

"Yesterday? Twenty-three days ago! Twenty-three days have gone by since the famous concert. But don't worry. I will tell you about it later."

"But I want to know!"

"It's all quite pleasant and innocent. And that you have got over your meningitis is also pleasant. But don't worry!"

He put more ice on my forehead, and insisted that I remain quiet. I fell asleep again. Two days later I was able to leave my bed, happy to feel that my legs could once again support me. And I called for the barber immediately, in order to have the illusion that I was resuming my normal life. And while I was under the razor, the doctor, pacing the room, decided to speak.

"Make sure you tell me the truth. Miss Eleanor will tell me everything today anyhow."

"Miss Eleanor left for England three weeks ago. She will never again return to Sicily. Despite her being both English and a theosophist, certain things will never be forgiven. But let me speak!"

"Is it bad then?"

"Not at all! Does it matter much, to a person like you, if you're the subject of the merry tale of a few thousand idlers for a while? So there's really no problem. The only problem is that, in the middle of the concert, yelling like a madman, you lugged the poor unconscious hunchback through the crowd."

I moved the razor away from me, as a precaution, and stood up, wringing my hands. I could neither laugh nor cry.

"It isn't true! Tell me that it isn't true!"

"It is absolutely true. And I won't describe the scene. There will be enough people eager to describe it to you, in all its particulars, until you will have had quite enough. But the particulars add more to Miss Eleanor's responsibility that to your discredit."

"Tell me that it isn't true!"

"That incomplete daughter of Albion received a well-deserved lesson. Every year she has woven some new romance, crowned by pleasant catastrophes. She has also had a few lovers, madmen who swear they have seen her with a Phidian[1] body. And I will make a confession. In the early days she tried the same game with me. But I have a healthy brain. And I've always seen her with two humps and as tall as a stool. With you, in the shape you were in, it was different."

I grabbed the razor, just as a joke.

"The only choices left to me are suicide or the cloister!"[2]

We laughed endlessly.

But, three days later, I left Magna Graecia forever.

---

1 A reference to the sculptor Phidias (fifth century BC) who, amongst other things, made two famous statues of Athena.

2 Likely a reference to Barbey d'Aurevilly's 1884 review of J.-K. Huysmans' *À rebours*, where he writes, ". . . logically, it only remains for the author to choose between the muzzle of a pistol or the foot of the cross."

A PARTIAL LIST OF SNUGGLY BOOKS

LÉON BLOY *The Tarantulas' Parlor and Other Unkind Tales*

S. HENRY BERTHOUD *Misanthropic Tales*

JAMES CHAMPAGNE *Harlem Smoke*

FÉLICIEN CHAMPSAUR *The Latin Orgy*

FÉLICIEN CHAMPSAUR
The Emerald Princess and Other Decadent Fantasies

BRENDAN CONNELL *Clark*

BRENDAN CONNELL *Unofficial History of Pi Wei*

ADOLFO COUVE *When I Think of My Missing Head*

QUENTIN S. CRISP *Aiaigasa*

QUENTIN S. CRISP *Graves*

LADY DILKE *The Outcast Spirit and Other Stories*

CATHERINE DOUSTEYSSIER-KHOZE *The Beauty of the Death Cap*

BERIT ELLINGSEN *Now We Can See the Moon*

BERIT ELLINGSEN *Vessel and Solsvart*

EDMOND AND JULES DE GONCOURT *Manette Salomon*

GUIDO GOZZANO *Alcina and Other Stories*

RHYS HUGHES *Cloud Farming in Wales*

J.-K. HUYSMANS *Knapsacks*

COLIN INSOLE *Valerie and Other Stories*

JUSTIN ISIS *Pleasant Tales II*

JUSTIN ISIS (editor) *Marked to Die: A Tribute to Mark Samuels*

JUSTIN ISIS AND DANIEL CORRICK (editors)
Drowning in Beauty: The Neo-Decadent Anthology

VICTOR JOLY *The Unknown Collaborator and Other Legendary Tales*

BERNARD LAZARE *The Mirror of Legends*

BERNARD LAZARE *The Torch-Bearers*

MAURICE LEVEL *The Shadow*

JEAN LORRAIN *Errant Vice*

JEAN LORRAIN *Masks in the Tapestry*

JEAN LORRAIN *Nightmares of an Ether-Drinker*

JEAN LORRAIN *The Soul-Drinker and Other Decadent Fantasies*

9 781943 813872